HOLD HANDS
IN THE
DARK

A DCI DANI BEVAN NOVEL

#7

D1617521

By

KATHERINE
PATHAK

≈

THE GARANSAY PRESS

Books by Katherine Pathak

The Imogen and Hugh Croft Mysteries:

Aoife's Chariot

The Only Survivor

Lawful Death

The Woman Who Vanished

Memorial for the Dead
(Introducing DCI Dani Bevan)

The Ghost of Marchmont Hall

Short Stories:

Full Beam

Mystery at Christmas Cottage

DCI Dani Bevan novels:

Against A Dark Sky

On A Dark Sea

A Dark Shadow Falls

Dark As Night

The Dark Fear

Girls Of The Dark

Hold Hands in the Dark

The Garansay Press

PROLOGUE

Crosbie Farm, West Kilbride, Christmas 1974

The tree was the best thing about the Faulkner family's Christmases. Magnus Faulkner always selected one of the most robust wee pines from the forest that lay on the fringes of their land.

With the tree freshly chopped and balanced in a bucket full of soil in the front room, Dale Faulkner carefully draped the string of multi-coloured lights across its prickly branches. The boy stood back and surveyed his handiwork.

'That's perfect, son,' his grandmother commented from the chair by the electric bar fire.

'I'm just gonna add a bit of tinsel,' Dale replied, fishing with his hand in the plastic bag of decorations his Ma had brought down from the attic that afternoon.

Vicki looked up from her Bunty annual, casting a critical eye over her little brother's display. 'Hmm, you'd better switch them on first. If one of the lights has blown you'll have to take it all off and start again.'

Dale nodded. His sister was right. He leant down behind the tree, feeling its pines prickling his face and the scent of the needles filling his nose as he fumbled to get the plug into its socket.

For a split second, the pretty little tree was lit up by a dozen multi-coloured fairy lights. Granny Lomas even had time to let out a little sigh of approval. Then they were plunged into darkness.

Dale was still crouched behind the tree. He nearly toppled the whole thing over with the shock of the sudden absence of light.

'Are you still there?' He cried out in alarm.

Vicki snorted an unpleasant laugh. 'Of course we

are, squirt. Where did you think we'd gone? Beamed up by the Starship Enterprise?'

'Maybe the fuse got blown,' Granny muttered. 'Those cheap lights are a menace.'

'I think it's just another power cut,' Vicki suggested boredly. 'Dale, go and fetch the candles from the kitchen, will you.'

'But I canae see a thing!' The boy's voice was shrill. The panic was washing over him in waves.

'There's no need to be a'feared, laddie,' his Granny soothed. 'We're surely used to this by now. We've been more without power than with it these past few months.'

'I know,' Dale sniffled. 'But Ma's not here. She knows how to light all the lamps and the fire and stuff. Dad doesn't bother coming back into the farmhouse when there's a power cut. He's got his torches to use out in the sheds.'

'Look,' Granny exclaimed. 'There's some moonlight coming in through the window. Your Ma will only be another hour or so.' She made her tone as gentle as possible. 'Come and gather around my chair. We'll do what we used to when the two of you were bairns.'

Dale extricated himself from behind the tree and crawled along the uneven wooden floor to sit beside her. To his surprise, Vicki slid off the sofa to do just the same.

'Now,' Granny said quietly. 'We shall hold hands in the dark. Then we will know we aren't on our own.'

'And will you tell us a story too?' Dale felt his worries melting away. He used to love this game as a bairn.

'Of course,' she replied.

While listening to Granny Lomas's tale about bombing raids and underground shelters, Dale concentrated on the sensation of her warm, bony hand in his. He could feel the roughness of her skin and the veins standing up very slightly on its surface. Vicki's hand was softer, her skin plump and springy.

Dale imagined this must be what it was like for blind people, who had to rely on their remaining senses to explore the world around them.

As if to test this theory, Dale began to hear a faint sound, just discernible above the lyrical rhythm of his Granny's clear voice. The sound was getting louder. It was coming from somewhere outside. Soon, he had tuned out the story altogether and was simply concentrating on those distant, strange noises.

There was something about the sounds that he recognised. Every atom of his being was straining to hear what was going on.

Then the shot came. It was so loud that the three of them automatically broke the circle and put their hands up to their ears to protect them. In that instant, Dale thought he must have been right – that the all-enveloping darkness had made their hearing supersensitive, so that the sudden sound assailed them like a physical blow.

Granny struggled to her feet. 'What in heaven's name was that?'

No one answered. Vicki had thrown her arms around her wee brother's shoulders and was gripping him tightly, as much for her own comfort as his. Granny said no more and appeared to be frozen to the spot.

A complete silence followed the crack of the gunshot and Granny's unanswered question. It was broken only by the sound of Dale's muffled but uncontrollable sobs.

Chapter 1

Richmond, Virginia, USA. Present day.

Sergeant Sam Sharpe tapped the final sentence into his report and fired it off to his superior officer. The Virginia PD detective had just turned fifty. He'd given over thirty years of service to the department. He could afford to take a comfortable retirement package at any time he liked. It was just a question of what he wanted to do next with his life.

Sam swept a hand through his thick hair, which possessed only a sprinkling of grey. He was heavily built and had a tendency to store fat. In recent months, Sharpe had been weight training, like he'd done in his youth, before Janie and the boys came along. Now his arms and torso were bulked up with muscle rather than excess flesh.

The sergeant was just packing up his bag to return to his city centre apartment for the evening when Detective Cassie Sanchez pushed through the doors and entered his floor. Sanchez was a lean woman in her late thirties, serious-minded and dedicated to the job.

'How can I help you, Sanchez?' Sam eyed her carefully. He could tell there was something wrong. The woman's dark brown eyes were darting from desk to desk, as if she were searching for somebody. 'Dale isn't here. He's on a callout.'

Sam knew that Sanchez and one of his best detectives had been an item for about a year now. Detective Dale Faulkner had been spilt from his wife for a long while and Sam was pleased he'd got together with such a level-headed woman like Cassie. He also happened to be convinced that the only relationship that could really work for cops was one with another cop.

The woman's attractive face began to crumple. 'I know, sir. We've been monitoring all the radio communications taking place on the Southside of the city down in Narcotics this evening. We intercepted somethin' –,' her voice cracked.

Sam got to his feet. 'What's happened Detective?'

Tears had escaped onto her cheeks. 'It's Dale. He and Gabe answered a domestic callout – the neighbours had heard screams, an argument-,'

'Yeah, I was here when they got the call.' Sam felt his stomach do a flip.

'Dale went into the house alone. I heard him tell Gabe to wait out in the car.'

'That's not proper procedure,' Sam mumbled, starting to get a really bad feeling about this.

'Dale was gone a good few minutes - ten maybe, fifteen at the most. Then Gabe clearly started to get worried about his partner 'cause he tried to radio Dale, but there was no answer.' Cassie put her hands up to cover her face. 'He's dead, Sergeant Sharpe! Dale's dead!'

Sam took a couple of steps forward and enveloped the distraught woman in his strong arms.

*

The name of this suburb had always reminded Sam of his ex-girlfriend, Dani. Midlothian lay to the west of Richmond, just south of the James River. The place had been named after its Scottish counterpart by the brothers who founded it as a coal-mining community 300 years earlier.

The mining industry was now long-gone from the area. In its place were pleasant suburban villas, highways and schools. It also happened to be where the Faulkner household was situated.

Sam pulled up outside a neat, detached house with gabled windows. He'd been there many times for dinner and barbecues when Dale and Toni had still been together. Only the Faulkners' youngest child, Grace, still lived at home with her Mom. The other two had finished college and were living in their own places.

There was an SUV parked up in the driveway. Sam took a deep breath before he rang the bell.

Toni pulled open the door very slowly. She was wearing a halter-neck top with a long, flowing skirt. Sam assumed she'd been out in the garden. Her eyes widened when she saw who was standing on her doorstep. 'You'd better come inside,' she said weakly.

Sam followed her into the kitchen. The back door was open onto the sweeping porch. He could make out a swing chair, positioned in the morning sunshine, with a paperback novel lying open on one of its cushions.

'I'm sorry to bother you at home, Toni. Would you mind taking a seat?'

The woman lowered herself slowly onto one of the kitchen chairs. Sam sat down opposite her.

'I can't tell you for how many years I dreaded this visit, Sam.' Toni's voice was distant and hesitant. 'But since Dale and I split, I honestly never thought about it again. I reckoned I didn't have to any longer, that I was free of the anguish.'

'I'm so sorry, Toni.'

'How did it happen?'

'There's going to be an internal inquiry into the incident. I can only tell you so much.'

Toni raised her gaze, looking quizzical. 'How come?'

Sam sighed heavily. 'A call was made to the

emergency desk late yesterday afternoon. There'd been reports of an attack on a woman inside of a house in a neighbourhood on the Southside of the city. Dale volunteered to go out there and take a look. Gabe went with him.'

'Detectives always go out in twos, don't they? You make it sound like Gabe's presence was an afterthought.'

Sam noted how perceptive Toni was. 'Yeah, you're right. I was there when Dale responded to the report. It was almost like if Gabe hadn't automatically got up to follow, Dale would have gone out alone.'

Toni shook her head. 'Well, that doesn't make much sense.' She gulped. 'What did they find there?'

'The address they'd been given was in a pretty shabby block. The house itself had some boarded up windows. There was no sign of the neighbours who'd called the disturbance in. Usually, one will come out onto the sidewalk when the cops show up. But there was nothin'.'

'They might have been scared.' Toni wanted to keep talking, to delay the inevitable.

'Sure, it's a possibility. Dale told Gabe to wait in the car. He patted his holster and then proceeded up to the front door.'

'Hang on – so Dale went in there *alone*?'

'Yeah, it's a breach of protocol. Gabe's facing a disciplinary charge. That's why an inquiry has been set up.'

'But if Dale *told* Gabe to stay put?'

Sam shrugged. 'It's early days, Toni. Gabe's still mightily shaken up. He sat in the car for about ten minutes, maybe twenty. He said the place was as quiet as the grave. He tried to radio Dale a couple of times and got no response. That's when he went in.'

Toni breathed back a sob.

'The door wasn't locked and the place was in

darkness. It didn't look like it had been lived in for years. Gabe kept calling out for Dale and there was no response. He was having trouble seeing where he was going until he spotted a light at the end of the corridor. He followed it to the kitchen, where a couple of candles had been lit inside old wine bottles. A back door out into a paved yard was swinging open, causing the flames to flicker violently. Then Gabe saw Dale. He was seated at the table. His body slumped against the back of the chair. Dale had a single bullet wound to the forehead. For what it's worth Toni, it would have been real quick. I don't believe he suffered. That's somethin' to tell the kids, sweetheart.'

Chapter 2

Pitt Street Police Headquarters, Glasgow.

Despite having worked at the Police Scotland HQ for over a decade, DCI Bevan had never been into this particular conference room before. It was located deep within the upper floors of the building, where only the most senior of the management honchos dwelt.

DCS Ronnie Douglas was chairing the meeting. He was a tall, imposing man in his early fifties with a head of thick, dark hair. His face was surprisingly unlined for a senior policeman but his countenance was as changeable as a steel girder. You never quite knew what was going through his head.

'With the sudden departure of Deputy Chief Constable Ross, the AC would like me to take on some additional responsibilities - just until his replacement can be found.'

Dani Bevan wondered if that replacement would be Douglas himself. If so, it would be one of the most meteoric career progressions she'd witnessed during her time on the force. The DCI remained silent. She knew that it was her operation into the murders of four young women in the 1970s that had led to the removal of DCC Ross. Dani had no desire to rock the boat any further.

'The AC has asked me to sweep a broom through the upper corridors of Pitt Street,' Douglas continued. 'Absolutely no one is to be above suspicion. I'm assuming it goes without saying that anything discussed in this room goes no further.' He fixed a menacing glare upon each person present. 'Good. It transpires that on a number of occasions, DCC Ross deliberately directed investigations away from his golfing pal, Gregory Suter – a man now awaiting trial for a series of sickening murders.'

'Did Ross know what Suter was up to?' Dani couldn't help but ask, her tone tinged with shock and incredulity.

Douglas shook his head slowly. 'We don't believe so. Otherwise, he'd be in the dock alongside Suter. It appears that Gregory worked very hard to develop close relationships with men in important positions. He used this influence to evade capture for so many years. It won't only be the erstwhile DCC who is tied up in this. There will be others. It's our job to flush out the rest.' The DCS scanned the faces before him once again, this time his expression was softer. 'Those of you seated around this table represent the only people within the walls of the Pitt Street station that I wholeheartedly trust, beyond the Assistant CC and the Chief Constable himself. Not least because we've had you all thoroughly vetted.' Just the tiniest hint of a wry smile played upon his thin lips.

'Do you want us to provide you with information, sir?' A DCI from the vice squad asked this question.

Douglas nodded. 'Trust nobody in your team. Believe me, Suter was handing out bribes like they were penny sweeties for the last four decades. His control runs deep within this force. *Anything* unusual needs to be reported back to me - immediately.'

Dani shifted uncomfortably in her seat. 'But this kind of witch-hunt is surely going to generate bad feeling within the ranks, Guv. Our teams operate on mutual support and trust.'

Douglas's forehead creased. 'The term witch-hunt, suggests that our suspicions are unfounded. I only wish that they were, DCI Bevan. The First Minister herself is launching an inquiry into the Suter case. A forty-year old miscarriage of justice is enough to bring down governments. We need to have cleared our division of dirty officers by the time these investigators start work, because if you think I'm an unfeeling bastard, wait till you meet that lot.'

Dani grimaced, nodding begrudgingly to her boss. In her heart she knew he was right. But Dani was still reluctant to imagine that anyone on *her* team would ever be in the pocket of a criminal. It was the Serious Crime Division who busted the case and exposed the miscarriage of justice, after all. But she needed to work with Ronnie Douglas, share information with him and learn to place her faith in his judgement, because the alternative just didn't even bear thinking about.

*

Dani called her team into their new de-briefing suite. It was one of the concessions she'd managed to gain from the DCS for their success on the Suter case. A gaggle of admin workers had been shifted into a broom cupboard somewhere to make the space available. But Dani struggled to care. They had too many pen-pushers at Pitt Street as it was.

'Tony MacRae's body was found on the steel hull of the ship he was helping to build on Friday morning, when the first of the workers began to clock into the yard.' Dani gestured towards a series of scene photographs, showing the man's injuries and the position of his body. 'The *post mortem* report indicates that death was caused by massive internal injuries corresponding to a rapid descent from 120 feet. This was the distance from the hull of the boat to the working platform we believe MacRae was standing on before the fall.'

'Any pre-fall injuries evident, Ma'am?' Asked DS Andy Calder.

'Not that the pathologist could identify. It was the

fracture of the upper spine that occurred as he hit the ground which killed him. The force pretty much severed his spinal column.'

'Then we're talking accidental death, Ma'am?' DS Alice Mann got to her feet. 'Shouldn't we be referring this to the Fiscal's office?'

Dani took a deep breath. 'The case landed on my desk because Mrs MacRae has been telling every reporter who'll listen, and there are plenty of those, that her husband was murdered by Hemingway Shipyards. She's written to the Chief Constable *and* the First Minister, making sweeping accusations about serious breaches of safety procedure at the company. In the current climate, we need to investigate this death like any other on our books.'

'So we may be looking at an incidence of corporate manslaughter?' DI Phil Boag suggested. 'In which case, we need to dig back into the shipyard's safety records, their employee accident and health reports, that kind of thing.'

'Aye, Phil. Can you and Andy make a start on that?'

Dani turned her head. 'Alice, I'd like you and DC Clifton to interview the wife. But make sure you're diplomatic about it. She needs to be confident that we're taking her allegations deadly seriously.'

Chapter 3

DC Dan Clifton drove along the north bank of the River Clyde into the busy centre of Partick. They followed the Dumbarton Road until the grand villas had fallen away to be replaced by the tattier post-war housing that Dan associated with this area.

The terraced property they stopped outside was more neatly kept than most on its street. Alice climbed out of the squad car first and approached the front door.

A woman in her early fifties answered.

She wasn't as the detectives had expected. Nancy MacRae was tall and slender, her wavy chestnut brown hair reaching her shoulders and her face lightly made-up and attractive.

'You'd better come away in,' the woman suggested, in a thick Glaswegian accent.

The officers were led into a bright kitchen extension at the rear. The vaulted ceiling let in a stream of natural light. Nancy moved towards a fancy looking kettle and flicked the switch.

They introduced themselves.

Alice asked, 'are you on your own?' She made the enquiry warily, not sure what kind of reception they were going to receive.

'I was offered family liaison, if that's what you're driving at, but I refused. The very last thing I want right now is a stranger in my house.'

'Aye, I can understand that. But a relative or a friend can often be a good companion to have during the first few days of a bereavement.'

Nancy's face creased into a tolerant smile. 'I'm certain you mean well, Detective Sergeant. But I'm not a great one for 'tea and sympathy', not when there's work to be done. I've been in this situation before. I won't do what my mother did.'

Dan crinkled his brow. 'How do you mean, Mrs MacRae?'

Nancy brought three mugs out of a cupboard. 'Don't tell me you haven't discovered who I am yet? And you people call yourselves detectives?' The woman chuckled humourlessly.

'You'd better enlighten us then,' Alice replied, equally dryly.

'My maiden name is Duff. My father was Alec Duff.'

This meant absolutely nothing to Alice Mann. Her expression remained blank. But Dan had recognised the name. He was searching around in his brain for the context.

Nancy filled a cafétiere with coffee. 'There was a time when my father's name would have been on the lips of every member of the polis in this city.'

Dan suddenly nodded his head in recognition. 'Alexander Duff, the General Secretary of the MWSD. My pa was a member, when he worked down at the docks for a wee while. Your father was a hero to him.'

Alice nudged his elbow, not liking to be left in the dark.

Dan turned towards his superior in rank. 'The Marine Workers, Shipbuilding and Designers Union. Mr Duff led the organisation during the seventies. He'd started out as a welder by trade.'

Nancy joined them at the table, setting down their drinks. 'Aye, he was a hero to a lot of people, until someone put a bullet in his heid.'

'It was during the early eighties, wasn't it?' Dan sipped the coffee, finding it was very good.

'February 1982. Ferris and Brewer's workers

were out on strike against the layoffs. Dad visited the picket line to lend his support. There was a big crowd. A shot suddenly rang out and my father fell to the ground. The bullet had hit him square to the temple. He died almost immediately.'

'Did they find the gunman?' Alice sat up straighter in her seat. This world was at one remove from her own experience. Her parents wouldn't have dreamt of joining a union, not in a million years. They'd always taken the side of the authorities if there was ever a strike.

Nancy nodded sadly. 'It was some poor idiot that the bosses had turned against his own kind, filling his head with bullshit about times changing and industries having to adapt. The man was desperate – his wife and kiddies were missing out on food due to the low levels of strike pay. Ferris and Brewer must have offered him some sort of pay rise if he broke the strike. In his muddled brain he blamed my father for the effects of the walkout. But we all knew who was *really* to blame.'

'The man served life for murder. I can't recall his name now.' Dan looked philosophical.

'Eddie Lambert. He did the bosses' bidding and got a prison sentence for the privilege. His weans were left destitute. And my Ma just sat back and took it. She never fought to bring the *real* culprits to justice.'

Alice leant forward, trying to appear sympathetic. 'And that's what you want to do for Tony now?'

Nancy brought her palm down hard on the table, some of the brown liquid spilling out of the cups. 'Don't patronise me, sweetheart. I was being beaten to the ground by riot shields when you were still in nappies.'

Dan raised his hand. 'Hold on, let's start over again, shall we? We've come here to listen to your side of things, Mrs MacRae. We only want to know what happened to your husband.'

Nancy breathed deeply, apparently calming herself down. 'Okay, fine.' She turned to Dan. 'But I'll only speak with you, alright? I want little Miss Silver-Spoon to wait outside.'

Dan shot a pleading glance at the DS.

Alice rose slowly to her feet. 'I'll be in the living room, if you need me.'

*

Within seconds, Nancy MacRae was like a different woman. Her tensed up body visibly relaxed and the lines on her face seemed to miraculously disappear.

'Can you talk me through your husband's movements on Thursday of last week?' Dan began gently.

'Tony was a foreman for the Hemingway Shipyard. They're the last of their kind operating on the Clyde. All of their workers are on temporary contracts. If the yard hasn't got any orders, the men don't have a job.'

Dan nodded encouragingly, thinking he could do without the polemic.

'Right now, the yard has a major contract to fulfil. It's like feast or famine with the management of that place. You're either getting your hours cut, or you're expected to work around the clock to meet some ridiculous deadline with no extra pay.'

'And on this occasion, Tony was working around the clock?' Dan didn't want to prompt, but he needed the bare facts, not a political sermon.

'Aye, that's right. He'd already done a full day's work on Thursday and come home for his tea. Then he abruptly gets up and says he's going back to the yard. There was some paperwork he needed to catch up on.'

'What time was this?'

'About half past seven. I went into the study to mark some essays. Before I even realised, it had turned eleven. That's when I called him, on the mobile.'

'Did you get an answer?'

Tears had sprung to her eyes. 'Yes, he said that he still needed to check on some of the work his men had done that day. Tony promised he wouldn't be much longer.' She sniffed noisily. 'So I went to bed. The next thing I knew, the phone was ringing. It just didn't stop until I pulled myself together and picked it up. One of Tony's team was on the other end of the line. He said there'd been an accident. They were waiting for an ambulance and could I go straight to the Infirmary and meet them there. At first, I didn't know who they were talking about. Then I glanced down at the empty space in the bed, next to where I'd just been lying. The light of dawn was filtering through the curtains. I realised that he hadn't come home. I knew my Tony was dead.'

Dan reached across and rested a hand on her arm. 'Would your husband often go up to the work platform on his own at night like that?'

She gazed down at the floor. 'It wasn't usually his job, but if he was worried that his men hadn't done the work right he'd wait until they'd gone home for the day to climb up and check.'

'He wasn't wearing a hard hat when he fell.'

Tears were dripping straight from her face onto the stone tiles, creating a tiny puddle. 'Tony didn't always put one on, not if he was simply performing an inspection. If he'd been with the workers, of course he would have. It was his responsibility to set a good example to the men.'

'Then isn't this just a terrible, horrible accident,

Mrs MacRae?'

Nancy whipped her head back up. 'I don't care what Tony was wearing or not wearing when he climbed up that platform. It was the pressure they were all under that made him go back to the yard that late. It was the *impossible* deadlines that were being set which meant his team cut corners and didn't finish the work properly. If the end product wasn't satisfactory it would be *Tony*, as the foreman, who'd be asked to leave, with no severance pay or notice because of those damned *zero hours* contracts they were all on. The management of Hemingway Shipyard caused my husband's death as surely as if the CEO had pushed Tony from that platform with his own bare hands.'

Chapter 4

The Scotstounhill flat was in darkness. Dani flicked on the lights and notched up the heating. It had been a while since she'd come home to an empty place. Her boyfriend, James, was back in Edinburgh for a few days, staying with his parents and visiting clients.

Dani had actually got used to the sounds and smells of dinner being on the go as she stepped over the threshold. It seemed petty and callous now to think that she had ever found it irritating and intrusive. Yet, as she padded her stockinged feet into the dark kitchen and slid a bottle of white wine out of its narrow shelf, Dani experienced the old tingle of anticipation. The feeling that she need not be answerable to another human being for at least eight hours and might do exactly as she wished.

The phone on the hall table began to chime and Dani recalled that this dream of protracted solitude had never actually been a reality.

'DCI Bevan,' she answered in a clipped tone.

'Oh, hi there Dani. I really hope I'm not interrupting your evening.'

'*Sam?*' It must have been at least two years since she'd heard Detective Sharpe's distinctive drawl.

'Err, yeah. I know it's been a while. I hear you're doing well. I've followed some of your recent cases on the international news sites.'

Dani had been caught off-guard. 'Thanks. So, how are you? Are the boys okay?'

'They're just fine. Jake's at College now. He's studying Stateside, so I get to see a lot more of him than I used to.'

'That's really great.' She frowned. 'What time is it

for you, are you calling from the department?'

There was a slight pause on the other end of the line. 'Actually, it's the same time as for you. I'm at the Hutchisons' place.'

'In Falkirk?'

'Yep.'

Dani ran a hand through her dark brown hair which she'd allowed to grow in recent months so that it now fell in neat waves to her shoulders. This statement had genuinely thrown her. 'Do you come to Scotland often?'

Sam chuckled. 'This is the first time I've been in the UK since the Richard Erskine case. But I'd been meaning to visit Bill and Joy for a while. I've been pretty damn useless at keeping in touch with them to be honest. Bill, on the other hand, writes to me often. His letters mean a lot.'

Dani had no idea that Bill kept up a link with her ex-lover in this way, he'd never mentioned it. But then Sam Sharpe *had* saved her friend's life. She supposed that created a bond. It would certainly mean something very profound to the Hutchisons, who set a great deal of store by that kind of thing since their own son had died in tragic circumstances several decades before.

'Look, I realise that me calling out of the blue like this is gonna come as a shock. But my reasons are purely professional, I promise. I could call you Ma'am, if it helps?'

Dani felt her mouth form a smile and the blood immediately rush to her cheeks. 'It really doesn't. Just tell me what this is all about.'

'A detective on my team, Dale Faulkner, was murdered when responding to a 911 call to a domestic disturbance last month.'

'I'm sorry.'

'Yeah, well, Dale left an ex, three kids and a

girlfriend to grieve for him. But somethin' about the callout just didn't add up, so I did some digging into his past. Turns out that Dale spent the first eight years of his life in your neck of the woods.'

'*Glasgow*?' Dani was curious now.

'West Kilbride, to be precise.'

Dani couldn't help but smile at the way Sam pronounced it. 'And you never knew he was Scottish.'

'The guy had a broader Virginian accent than I do. I suppose his family had been in the state so long that he just adapted to the ways of the locals.'

'You must have found out something significant for your investigations to have brought you all the way over here.'

'Yeah, you could say that. But I think it would be best if we met and discussed this face-to-face – if that wouldn't be a problem, of course?'

'Okay, let's meet. I don't see any reason why that should be a problem at all.'

*

DI Phil Boag and DS Andy Calder stood before Dani in her tiny office. Both men had gained promotions within the last year. In each case, the DCI believed they were richly deserved. This belief didn't prevent her from feeling the pang of regret and frustration that her own application to become a superintendent had been turned down.

'The Hemingway Shipyard has experienced five accidents in the past year,' Phil began, tapping at the screen of his leather bound tablet.

'Is that a lot, compared to other companies?' Dani leant her elbows on the desk.

'There *are* no other similar companies to compare

it to,' Andy added bitterly. 'Hemingway's is the last operational shipyard on the Clyde.'

'But having said that,' Phil chipped in, 'the health and safety department didn't think it was anomalous. In each case, human error on the part of the employee was to blame. All the proper procedures were in place, so the company weren't found liable.'

'Any fatalities in recent years, other than Tony MacRae?'

'No, Ma'am. But back in 2010, one of the welders broke his back and ended up in a wheelchair.'

'Another fall?' Dani's interest had definitely been piqued.

Andy stepped forward. 'I spoke to the guy on the phone, Ma'am. He seemed almost cagey about the whole incident. He claimed that he'd gone beyond the barrier he was supposed to, in order to reach an area he felt needed repair. That's when he lost his footing. But the way he told it, sounded like he was reading out a written statement.'

Dani pursed her lips. 'You think he may have received a payoff from Hemingways to give that story?'

Andy nodded. 'I reckon so. The Union's got no power in the sector any longer. The employees are pretty much operating at the whim of the management.'

Phil looked sceptical. 'The CEO I spoke with sounded reasonable. He said their accident reports were available to the public to view at any time. We'd need several sworn statements of negligence in order to even consider pursuing a charge of corporate manslaughter.'

Dani nodded. 'Clifton and Mann picked up some interesting info from the widow. I've sent them out to interview a few more witnesses before we drop the case entirely. Let's give Hemingways something to sweat about for a couple more days. I don't want them to feel like they've been let off the hook just yet.'

Chapter 5

It had been several months since Dani had visited the Hutchisons in Falkirk. Their detached property, located within a quiet, modern estate was exactly as she'd last seen it; the front garden neatly tended and the windows sparkling clean.

It was Joy who answered the door. 'DCI Bevan! How wonderful to see you. My, you've changed ever such a lot. Your hair is much more, err, - *feminine*, I suppose would be the word.'

Dani smiled graciously, knowing that her friend wasn't intending to be unkind. The detective realised her previous style must have appeared a little severe to those outside the force. But fitting in with her peers on the squad didn't seem quite as important to her now as it once did. 'How are the family?' She enquired, with genuine interest.

Joy took Dani's coat and led her along the corridor to the sitting room. 'Louise and the boys have settled comfortably into their new place. They've got a terraced house in Bathgate. They're not too far from us.'

Dani nodded politely, but had partially stopped listening to Joy's words. She could see her old friend and colleague Sam Sharpe, standing in the centre of the lounge with his back to the door, apparently deep in conversation with Bill. His profile was still as broad as when she'd previously encountered him but it was different somehow – more defined and muscular.

The man turned as he heard voices approaching.

The moment that Dani was dreading had finally arrived. Sam cracked that wide, disarming smile; the one which had the disturbing capability of utterly transforming his less than handsome face and lighting up a room like a hundred watt bulb.

'Dani! Great to see you again!' He reached out a large hand and shook hers vigorously. 'Hey, are you alright? You look a little pale.'

Dani managed to regain her poise. 'I'm fine, I've just been up since early this morning, that's all. No time for breakfast.'

'Oh my goodness,' Joy declared. 'I shall dish up lunch immediately, then.'

Bill stepped forward and scooped the detective into an embrace. 'Good to see you again, my dear. I think you look terrifically well, especially considering you've recently taken on the Scottish justice system and won!'

Dani chuckled, allowing her host to guide them towards the dining room. 'That's a bit of an overstatement.'

'To bring to light a miscarriage of justice that was forty years old and secure a conviction against a powerful businessman with connections to the very highest echelons of the Scottish establishment is no mean feat, lassie.'

Sam took a seat opposite her. 'Yeah, I did read you'd been busy.'

Dani shook out a napkin. 'Well, I don't work alone, as you well know. My team played as much of a part in that investigation as I did. In fact, it was young Alice Mann who found out the identity of the real killer of those girls. She's got a brilliant future ahead of her.'

Sam narrowed his blue eyes, sensing something different about his ex-lover. She no longer appeared to possess the drive and determination to succeed in the job that he remembered. To him, she was also looking fantastic. Her hairstyle was softer and although her face was pale and the DCI was obviously beat, from what he could tell, Dani had filled out a little, and in all the right places.

Dani glanced up at Sam, meeting his eye for the first time since her arrival. 'I'm really sorry about your colleague. I know how responsible we feel towards our team as a commanding officer.'

'Thanks.' The American sighed. 'Dale was also a good friend. When he was still living with his wife and I was with Jane and the boys we hung out together a lot. Family barbecues and that kinda thing.'

Joy entered with the serving plates, but said nothing to interrupt.

'Our kids were friends too. I went to see Toni after Dale had been killed and I'd done some digging into his past. His own wife of twenty years had no idea Dale was born in Scotland and spent pretty much the first decade of his life here. Doesn't that strike you as weird?'

Dani crinkled her brow, allowing herself some thinking time whilst she dug into the roast dinner. 'It's very unusual. He must have possessed dual nationality. What did his passport say? Are there any close relatives left in Richmond to tell you more?'

'The guy turned out to have two passports, one for the US and one for the UK.' Sam put down his cutlery and gazed around the table. 'We found his original passport in a wallet in his police locker, of all places. Holding it in my hand was one of the freakiest experiences I've ever had. It was issued in July 1976. The photo inside was of Dale as a goofy little kid, with gaps in his teeth and dessert-bowl hair.'

'To renew the passport, Dale would have had to return to the UK and present himself to the appropriate government building,' Bill added.

'There's no evidence he ever came back to Scotland since his family emigrated to the States. We couldn't find any living relatives in the US, either. His folks passed away in the late nineties. I never met them.'

'Why do you think the man's Scottish origins have anything to do with his death?' Dani was intrigued.

'The first thing my team did after Dale got shot in that dump on the Southside of the city was to look into who owned the place. The landlord was living in the Midwest somewhere but he gave us a list of tenants. It'd been standing empty for several months, but its most recent occupants were a middle aged couple called McNeil. They'd given the owner a social security number, so we traced them through that.'

'Do you think this couple still had access to the house?'

'We didn't know what the hell to think if I'm honest, Dani. But it was the only damn lead we had. It turns out the McNeils were schoolteachers, who worked at a couple of public high schools in the centre of the city until the spring of 2014. No one's heard from them since. I spoke to the principal of one of the schools. What he recalled most about the husband, John, was how attached he was to his Scottish heritage. The pair were both true blue Americans, but they made a big thing of having ancestors over here.'

'Did the principal know whereabouts they hailed from?'

'Yeah, you see that's the thing. Mr McNeil was a geography teacher. He had a map on the wall of his classroom with his ancestral hometown encircled with thick red ink. It was Portencross, West Kilbride. Just like Dale Faulkner and his family.' Sam crossed his arms over his broad chest. 'Now, don't tell me that's a coincidence, DCI Bevan, 'cause I just ain't gonna believe you.'

Chapter 6

Sam had left Dani with plenty to think about. He'd made copies of all his investigative notes and passed them onto her. The file lay on the passenger seat beside the DCI as she drove back to Glasgow.

James had left her a message. His mother was ill again and he was going to stay on at their home in Leith until she was a little better. James's sister was a high profile defence advocate in Edinburgh and could never take time away from her work. It fell to the Irvings' youngest child to rally round in a crisis. Dani knew her boyfriend could work easily from there. His current clients were based in the capital anyway.

Dani still felt uneasy about his absence. She could really do with James to be at home, providing his usual steady, reassuring presence, to prevent her mind from dwelling on Sam Sharpe. Nostalgia was a powerful emotion, she knew that. Dani couldn't afford to mistake the feeling for anything else.

The DCI was relieved when a call came through on her hands free. It was from DS Alice Mann.

'Afternoon, Alice. What have you got for me?'

'Dan and I interviewed a member of Tony McRae's team, Ma'am. He claims that the platform Tony fell from was supposed to be out of bounds. One of the protective barriers was damaged. He says the foreman knew about this. He can't understand what McRae would have been doing up there on Thursday night.'

'Is he willing to provide a formal statement?'

'I've got it right here, Ma'am.'

'Good work. Tell Phil to get back onto the CEO

and confront him with it. The director made no mention of the faulty safety equipment when he was first questioned. We'll also have to get statements from all the men who were working on that ship. If the others find out that one of their colleagues is willing to talk, there may just be some more brave souls prepared to come forward.'

'Aye, Ma'am. DC Clifton is already on it.'

*

Dani pulled the door to her office closed and opened the file from the Richmond Police Department. She could almost smell the strong coffee and taste the sweet pastries that had contributed to its compiling. But perhaps that wasn't how Sam worked any longer. It had certainly looked as if the detective had recently been on one hell of a health kick.

She focussed her attention on Dale Faulkner instead. Sam had really done his research on the guy. But then Dani knew from her own experience how driven Sam had been to bring the murderer of a US citizen to justice. It was how she'd met the detective in the first place. Faulkner was also a member of Sam's squad, and a good friend.

Dale was born in the Glasgow Infirmary in 1967. His family rented Crosbie Farm, near Farland Head in West Kilbride. The Faulkners had farmed the land for three generations. But in the summer of 1976, when Dale was nine years old, the family moved to Midlothian, in the Petersburg region of Richmond, Virginia.

Dani looked up from the notes. It struck her as poignant that the Faulkners had chosen to emigrate to a place with a Scottish name. Perhaps it allowed the family to feel like the move was less of a wrench.

Somehow, it made the DCI sense that the relocation wasn't entirely what the family wanted. They were trying to cling to a vestige of what they'd left behind.

As she read on, however, the motivation became clearer. The Midlothian area was named by the Wooldridge brothers, who had settled there three hundred years earlier. They established a coal-mining and farming community in Midlothian, Virginia to match the region's namesake back in Scotland. Coal-mining wasn't practised in the area by the seventies but the Faulkners had set up a modest smallholding, making the most of the preponderance of creeks and fertile land.

Dani flicked back through the pages to Sam's earlier notes. Magnus and Susan Faulkner had two children. Victoria was born in 1965 and would have been eleven at the time of the move. But there was no mention of her living at the farm in Virginia. Dani lifted the phone on her desk and called Sam's mobile.

'Hey, how can I help?'

'What happened to Dale's sister? There's no record of her living in the United States.'

'No, she never went with the rest of the family. The elder daughter stayed in Scotland with her grandmother, according to your social security registers. I assumed they didn't want to disrupt her schooling in the UK.'

'She never went out to join them later? I think that's odd, don't you? How old would Victoria be now?'

'She'll be fifty, maybe fifty-one. Same age as me.'

'And as far as we know, she's never lived outside Scotland?' Dani drummed her fingers on the desk. 'It might be useful to try and pin down an address. Let's have a little chat with Victoria Faulkner, if we can.'

Chapter 7

Phil and Andy stood in a plush foyer, where framed photographs of imposing battleships and cruise liners hung on every wall.

The receptionist finally nodded towards a closed door at the end of the corridor. Phil entered first, taking a chair at the shiny desk.

'DI Boag and DS Calder, pleased to meet you. I'm Raymond Hemingway, CEO of Hemingway Shipyards.'

The man was thin and balding, but the expensive suit and dark rimmed designer glasses gave him gravitas.

'Thank you for sparing us your time,' Phil began. 'I know you must be busy.'

Calder cleared his throat. He didn't know why his colleague had to be so damned ingratiating.

Hemingway formed a smile. 'We're always willing to help the authorities.'

Andy nearly snorted out a laugh. Fortunately, he was able to hold it back.

'We have spoken with a number of your workforce, Mr Hemingway. Some new evidence has come to light as a result,' Phil continued.

The smile died on the man's lips. 'Oh, yes?'

The DI glanced at his tablet. 'Platform 12b, the one that Tony McRae fell from, we have been informed that it was out of bounds to the workforce.' He glanced up. 'You didn't mention this before, when we spoke on the phone.'

Hemingway shifted in his seat. 'I wasn't aware that it was. I'd have to check with the safety crew. They make those kinds of decisions.'

'We've done that already, sir,' Andy chipped in. 'The safety manager designated the area dangerous to enter at the beginning of this month. He sent the information to you in an email dated the 3rd March.'

The CEO narrowed his eyes. 'These routine reports go through my PA. She will have filed the information appropriately, I'm sure. At my level, I don't always become aware of every single detail of what goes on within the shop floor, as it were.'

'Okay. So you claim you didn't know that the platform was unsafe?' Andy leant in close enough to smell the man's aftershave.

Hemingway blinked a couple of times before answering. 'No, I did not, although McRae was working on the boat outside of his designated hours, Detective Sergeant. Our handbook clearly states that this nullifies our responsibility towards his safety. Our lawyers are very certain about this.'

Andy nodded amenably. 'Yes, of course. But *our* lawyers say that if it's found that McRae felt pressurized into working long hours for fear of his job then that small print might just not be worth the paper it's written on.'

The CEO's face reddened. 'I'm not sure exactly how you would go about proving such a thing.'

'Oh, witness statements from your employees, their relatives, medical reports and mounting incidents of stress-related illness amongst the staff. The whole investigation could drag on for months.' Andy sat back and folded his arms across his chest, giving the impression of making himself very comfortable in the leather seat.

'We do appreciate your cooperation thus far.' Phil's voice sounded strained. 'But we're going to need further access to the site. Our techs only did a preliminary examination of the spot where Tony fell. We will now need to look closer.'

'Fine.' Hemingway threw a hand up into the air dismissively. 'Send in whoever you choose. But I won't stop production on their account. I need to get this ship out to the Middle East by the end of next week. The death of Tony McRae, however unfortunate, is not going to stop us.'

*

Phil strode ahead to the car, climbing into the driving seat and slamming the door. He said nothing until Andy was seated beside him and they were pulling out of the carpark.

'I thought we decided that *I* was going to lead the interview?'

Andy shrugged his shoulders. 'I wanted to push the conversation along a bit faster.'

'I was building up to confronting him with the more tricky questions. There was no need to go blustering in like a bull in a china shop. Now Hemingway is totally hostile. He isn't going to cooperate willingly with us in future.'

Andy grunted. 'He was hardly doing that anyway. The guy was bullshitting us. *Of course* he knew that platform was unsafe. It's the typical corporate response to claim you never received the email. These bastards are world champions at arse covering.'

Phil sighed. 'It's part of our job to be even-handed. We can't assume the company's guilt whilst we're still investigating the accident. As a senior officer, you should know that.'

Andy twisted in his seat. He noticed how hard his friend was gripping the wheel. Phil was seriously pissed off. 'I know you haven't spent much time in the field up to now, what with you being the primary carer to the girls and all that, but myself and the

DCI have a certain way of doing things. That's how I always interview one of the bad guys and believe me, Hemingway is definitely one of the bad guys. They sell warships to foreign dictators for Christ's sake!'

To Calder's great surprise, Phil abruptly brought the car to a halt at the side of the road. A van shot past them at speed, narrowly missing the wing mirror and blaring its horn in the process.

The DI turned to face him. His expression steely. 'Look, I realise you're used to working with the boss. And you and she have a way of doing things. But I'm the superior officer now. DCS Douglas has partnered us up and I'm determined to make it a success. Bevan liked to give you free reign, but I swear to God Andy, if you undermine me like that again in an interview I'm going to take it upstairs. Not to Dani, or even Douglas, but straight to the new DCC. Your glory days are over Calder. It's time to knuckle down and play ball, just like the bloody rest of us.'

Chapter 8

It was getting late. Dani was just considering fixing herself some dinner when the doorbell rang. She padded down the hallway and peered through the spyhole. It was Andy.

Dani opened up. 'Is everything okay?'

'At home, sure. Carol knows where I am. In fact, it was her who told me to come and speak with you.'

The DCI was intrigued. She stood back and allowed her friend to enter.

Andy breezed through the small flat to the dark kitchen, eyeing his surroundings as he passed. 'Is James the only one allowed to switch on the lights?'

Dani chuckled. 'I hadn't noticed how late it had got. I was about to make some food, actually.'

'Please don't mind me, go ahead. I ate with Carol and Amy hours ago. But a glass of wine wouldn't go amiss.'

Dani poured them both a glass of red. 'So, what's the problem?'

'Phil Boag.'

Dani crinkled her brow. 'Has something happened with the girls?'

'Naw, nothing like that. He just really lost it with me today, after we had our meeting with Hemingway at his office.' Andy recounted the events, word-for-word.

Dani busied herself at the stove for a few minutes, mulling the incident over before she responded. 'I suppose he had a point. Perhaps I indulged you a little bit when we were on the job. It was because I genuinely believed your methods worked. But then I don't have a bloke-sized ego. I never thought Phil did either, but then we didn't reckon on him having an affair and kicking Jane out. It's no surprise he wants to let you know who's of the higher rank. He was setting down a marker.'

Andy took a swig of Merlot. 'Yeah, I totally understand that. But there's more. It bugged me that Phil was so soft on Hemingway. It got me thinking.'

'Phil has a gentle manner, we've always known that. His strength is in the thoroughness of his background checks and paperwork. As far as working in the field is concerned, he'll quickly learn how to bust some balls.' Dani fried a chicken breast with an assortment of vegetables in a pan, feeling unconcerned. When she turned round to dish up, Andy's serious expression worried her.

'Phil left his tablet computer on the desk when he went to lunch. It was logged onto his bank details page. I checked out the previous month's transactions on his account.'

'You'd no authorisation to do that. If Douglas finds out, you're history.'

He nodded gravely. 'Yeah, but once the seed of doubt was planted, I had to see for myself.'

Dani dropped into the seat opposite. 'And?'

'Well, you know what it's like for Phil at the moment. He's got an ex-wife in a fancy flat on the Southside, a new wife installed at their house in Pollockshaws and Sorcha is in her first year at St Andrews. The guy has got some major financial responsibilities to shoulder right now.'

Dani didn't like the sound of this. She was shovelling the food into her mouth, but it barely tasted of anything.

'A deposit of £5,000 went into his account three days ago.'

'Do you *seriously* think that Phil is taking

backhanders from Hemingway Shipyards?'

'I've been talking it through with Carol for the last couple of hours. We couldn't come up with any other explanation.'

'Can the bank trace where the money came from?'

'I called them up this afternoon. I said I was from the fraud squad, performing random checks on larger than normal transactions. According to the cashier, the money was deposited by way of an envelope full of fifties passed over the counter at the West Princes Street branch on Monday.'

'Shit.' Dani put down her fork and lifted the wine glass. 'Then why put it into his account at all? If the money is dodgy, Phil would know we might check. We'd be able to get a court order no problem.'

Andy shrugged his shoulders. 'Perhaps he doesn't think we *will* check. Let's face it, the last person we'd ever believe was bent at the Pitt Street station is Phil 'saintly' Boag.'

The DCI thought about the instructions she'd been given by DCS Douglas at their confidential meeting. This was exactly the kind of evidence that her boss wanted brought to his attention immediately.

'For the time being, don't mention this to anybody at Pitt Street and don't confront Phil with what you know.'

Andy nodded, relieved to have dumped this particularly thorny problem on someone else.

'But I want you to keep a very close eye on him. Make a note of who he calls, what questions he asks witnesses and who he meets. Let's make sure we're absolutely certain about this before we drop our old friend in the crap.'

Chapter 9

Dani had arranged to meet Sam Sharpe on Kennedy Street in Glasgow, outside the impressive stone curved frontage of the St Mungo Academy of Music.

The American detective was late so Dani bought herself a cappuccino from a stall and sat on a bench where she could listen to the distant rumble of the M6. Finally, she saw him step out of a cab and jog towards her. He wore a thick padded jacket, despite the weather seeming quite mild to the DCI.

'Sorry, Dani. I got held up. Bill and Joy insisted on driving me to the station. We took a couple of sight-seeing detours along the way.' He gave her a crooked grin.

'Not a problem. I can imagine the scenario well.'

Sam sat on the bench beside her. She could feel the heat from his body warming her leg. 'It didn't take long for me to find out that Victoria Faulkner is now known as Vicki Kendrick. She teaches here at the College of Music.'

'Wow. Do you think she knows her brother is dead?'

'I'm not sure. Did any member of your department inform her?'

Sam shook his head. 'Nope. I didn't even know she existed until a few days back. Because she'd never followed her family to the States, I kinda supposed she was dead, maybe. The lady was certainly off the scene.'

'That's true. She'd been off the scene for nearly forty years, as far as the Faulkner family were concerned. But in Scotland the woman is actually quite well known. Vicki Kendrick is a renowned concert pianist. Even *I've* heard of her and I'm no connoisseur of classical music. She's been on television a lot and toured the world. According to her website, she played at Carnegie Hall last year.'

'So, she was in NYC. Do you think she visited Dale in Virginia whilst she was there? He never once mentioned he had a famous sister. Geez, you'd think he'd be proud of it.'

'Vicki has travelled all around the world during her career. It seems incredibly odd that she never visited her family in Richmond. It's not like she didn't have the resources to do so.'

'Then the woman lacked the inclination to see her folks. The question is, *why?*' Sam stood up. 'Let's go right ahead and ask her, shall we?'

*

The inside of St Mungo's was just as impressive as the exterior. A flight of sweeping stone steps disappeared up into the second floor. Dani could see that a series of assembly halls and practice rooms populated the ground level.

A receptionist called up to Vicki Kendrick's office. She supplied the detectives with a map printed onto a folded leaflet to help them find where they were going. The place was a maze of echoey corridors and marble pillars, each one identical to the last. Eventually, they found the room which boasted Ms Kendrick's name on a plaque on the door.

'Come in!' A voice called out brusquely.

Dani entered first, holding out her warrant card and introducing herself and Sam.

The woman remained seated. Dani had seen the musician a couple of times on chat shows but in the flesh, Vicki appeared small and vulnerable. Her face was expertly made up and her hair a very natural looking deep auburn.

'Please take a seat. How may I help you?'

The accent was definitely refined Scots, Dani noted, but her intonation so soft that the effect was fairly generic. She could have originated anywhere in the western world. The DCI could tell that her companion was struggling to connect this rarefied music teacher with his dead friend.

'Ms Kendrick, is it correct that you were born Victoria Mary Faulkner, at the Glasgow Infirmary in the October of 1965?'

'Yes, that is correct. Although, I don't tend to broadcast my age, Detective Chief Inspector. As a woman in the performing arts you learn very quickly to be a little vague about the specifics.'

'And your parents were Magnus and Susan Faulkner, resident of Crosbie Farm, West Kilbride at the time of your birth.'

She crinkled her brow, displaying the tell-tale lines that revealed more than a false birth date could ever hope to obscure. 'Why is this important?'

Sam leant forward, resting his elbows on his knees. 'I'm very sorry to inform you, Ma'am, but your brother, Dale, passed away in the line of duty a month back. I knew him well and he served his adopted country with bravery and honour.'

Dani examined her reaction closely.

Vicki put a hand to her face and abruptly stood up, moving towards the tall window behind her desk and gazing out at the view of the city it afforded. They allowed the woman a few moments to compose herself.

'When had you last seen your brother, Ms Kendrick?' Dani asked gently.

Vicki turned back to face them. Looking pale, but with no tears having been shed, she replied quite simply, 'the 25th July, 1976.'

Chapter 10

Vicki Kendrick had finally ordered up some coffee for the detectives and moved them over to a soft seating area in the far corner of the office.

'Did you know Dale well?' The woman asked hesitantly, stirring a sachet of sweetener into her drink.

Sam nodded. 'He was a friend and colleague of mine for over twenty years. Dale was a very good cop and a great dad. He wasn't such a success as a husband, but then he sure wasn't alone in that.'

Dani shot him a sideward glance, but Sam's expression was jovial enough.

'So, there are children?' Vicki was struggling even to make eye contact with her visitors.

'Kyle, he's twenty six and the oldest. Then there's Lilly, she's twenty four and Grace, who is eighteen. They're all grown up now but lived with their mom following the split. Dale was close to all three. They're great kids.'

Dani shuffled forward. 'Is there a reason why you lost contact with your parents and brother?'

Vicki shrugged her narrow shoulders. 'When Dad decided that we should move away from the farm I was eleven years old and Dale was eight. Music was already a major part of my life. I'd won a scholarship to a private school in Glasgow that had fantastic facilities for the arts. My parents made the decision that I would stay in Scotland with my grandmother and continue my education here. It proved to be the right choice.' The woman gestured to her ornate surroundings, as if to illustrate the point.

'But I don't see why that meant you couldn't still visit your family in the holidays?' Dani was genuinely puzzled.

'Virginia is a very long way away and it felt like a million miles in the late seventies. We had little money for air fares in those first few years. I got wrapped up in my playing and began performing at the age of fourteen, the practice was continual. I was close to my gran. It didn't seem necessary to dwell on the past.' Vicki put the china cup to her lips, preventing any further discussion on the subject.

'It doesn't appear worth asking then, if you knew of any reason why someone would want your brother dead, as you've had no contact with him in forty years.'

Vicki shook her head. 'I really couldn't say. I'd have thought his death would more likely have something to do with him being a detective than with his life here in Scotland. Dale was only a little boy when he left.'

'Did your grandmother keep in contact with your parents, after they moved to America?' Dani was determined to persist with this line. She found the way the family had split up distinctly odd.

Vicki appeared uncomfortable. 'I suppose she must have done, with my mother, at least. But we never discussed it. Every family has their own way of dealing with difficult situations - that was ours.'

Sam stood up, indicating that the questioning was over. He put out a hand and shook hers warmly. 'Thank you for your cooperation, Ms Kendrick. When we've got the investigation completed, I'll send you the details of your brother's funeral. I really hope you can come.'

*

The detectives found a nearby café and took a window seat.

'Well, that was weird.' Sam ordered more coffees, with accompanying pastries this time.

'Vicki described the situation that evolved between her and her parents as *difficult.* I wonder what she meant by that.'

'If the family were forced to move to the States for financial reasons, but Vicki chose to stay behind, then that would have caused a serious rift. There would've been resentment on both sides.'

'But enough to mean there was no contact between a little girl and her mum, dad and brother for all those years? It just doesn't feel right.'

'No, it doesn't. But like the woman said, every family deals with this stuff differently.' Sam offered the DCI a slice from an impressive looking cream cake.

'Thanks.' Dani discovered she was starving and gratefully tucked in.

'We're judging those folk by our own standards. Hell, I can hardly comment. My boys are in Vancouver for Christ's sake.'

'But you visit them loads and speak every few days. This situation with the Faulkners is quite different. Vicki had been to America dozens of times with her performances, but never once looked up her parents. Now they're all dead and it's too late.'

'Yeah, it's a tragedy whichever way you look at it.'

'And Vicki was very quick to suggest that her brother's murder had nothing to do with his past here in Scotland.'

'Well, she had a pretty good point there. What could the eight year old Dale Faulkner have done, growing up in a remote farm in West Kilbride that got him executed at gunpoint, three and half thousand miles away and near as dammit forty years later?' Sam's expression was incredulous.

Dani said nothing. Slowly lifting her cup and washing down the sweet, delicious pastry, she was deep in her own thoughts.

Chapter 11

Just as Hemingway had threatened, work was carrying on as usual in the huge hanger of the yard where the new warship was being constructed.

Dani had accompanied her colleagues to the accident site. They had brought a tech team with them, who were currently re-examining the platform from which Tony MacRae fell to his death.

The DCI gazed around her in wonderment. The workers on platforms, way up the side of the enormous steel funnels looked like tiny wee ants in the distance. She was amazed by the sheer size of the operation.

Andy noticed her interest in their surroundings. 'Just imagine, Ma'am, there were shipyards exactly like this one, up and down the Clyde after the war. It's a tragedy that a whole industry was wiped out so quickly.'

Dani glanced at him. 'Do you have a connection to the shipyards?'

Andy shrugged. 'My Da' had a few cousins who worked on the big ocean liners back in the fifties. They were both involved in the walk-outs that took place during the late sixties.'

Phil tutted under his breath. 'Those men signed their own death warrants,' he muttered.

Andy spun round. 'What do you mean by that, *sir*?'

'Well, when folk are trying to cope without power for three days a week and piles of rubbish are lying around the streets, twitching with rats, public opinion is hardly going to be sympathetic to yet more industrial action. They actually made it easier for the government to shut those shipyards down.'

Dani could see that Andy's face had reddened with anger.

'Jimmy Reid's 'work-ins' did the opposite of that. His union men made sure they completed orders and kept tight discipline. The public were totally on side. Even Heath's government in '72 had to give in eventually and keep the Govan yards open.' The DS had his fists clenched down by his sides.

'Only for a short while. They were simply delaying the inevitable.' Phil petulantly kicked the pointed toe of his shiny shoe against a crack in the concrete floor. 'My parents recall that era very well. It was a difficult time for most hard-working Scots. My old grannie nearly froze to death in her bed one night, when there was no electricity for the heaters.'

Dani held up a hand. 'I don't quite see where this discussion is going to get us. We're here to find out what happened to Mr MacRae, not recreate the class conflicts of the seventies.'

'Tony's father-in-law was Alec Duff, one of the most prominent union men of his generation. Perhaps that had something to do with the foreman's death?'

Dani shook her head. 'I don't think so Andy, the power of the unions is long gone in this profession. It doesn't sound like Tony was a rabble-rouser. He was desperate to fulfil this order and keep his job.'

One of the techs clambered down from the platform and approached the officers. 'We can see where the scaffolding had become unsafe, Ma'am. A metal clip had snapped right in two, but it's been fixed recently. One of the workers showed us where a new clip had been secured over the broken piece. He said it was done yesterday.'

'So, our *friend* Raymond Hemingway has been tampering with the scene,' Andy added with venom.

Dani shot a glance at Phil, to see how he would react to this. The DI's expression remained impassive. She turned back to address the technician. 'Finish up with your evidence gathering, will you, Todd? Then we can get back to Pitt Street and send any samples to the lab. We'll let the management at Hemingways squirm for a week or so longer whilst we await the results. Then I think we've done all we possibly can for poor Mrs MacRae.'

*

Dani had been keeping a close eye on Phil all day but couldn't fault his actions. Everything was done by the book, as it always was with the DI. He certainly was the last person she would ever suspect of being corrupt. She and Andy had known the man for nearly fifteen years. He wasn't a working class warrior like Calder but Phil had his principles nonetheless.

With James out of the flat, Dani filled her evening reading an online biography of Alexander Duff, Nancy MacRae's father, on her laptop.

Duff had been born on the Southside of Glasgow during the Great Depression of the 1930s. His father had served in the navy during the Second World War and was a welder by trade. Alec followed in his father's profession and worked for several of the large shipbuilding firms in the sixties before becoming a shop steward in the Marine Workers, Shipbuilders and Designers Union. Duff was known for his toughness and staunch principles, earning him the role of union secretary in '72. This was the position Alec had held until his murder at the Ferris and Brewer strike in '82.

Dani had been too young to remember the news

coverage at the time, but had certainly watched documentaries about Duff since his death. He was gunned down by a shipworker at Ferris Brewer called Eddie Lambert, who'd been driven half mad by trying to support his large family on strike pay.

Lambert went into hiding after the shooting but was found by police at the home of an associate in Govan a week later. The man was convicted of murder in the spring of 1983. He died of lung cancer in Barlinnie in '98.

She shook her head solemnly. The entire situation struck her as tragic. These men were fighting to cling onto an industry that was doomed. The British government in the eighties was hell-bent on closing the yards. Just like the miners in '84, these workers were fighting a futile battle. It was the families who suffered most. Whether it was a battle that still needed to be fought depended upon your view of history.

Dani finished her glass of wine and stood up, deciding she may as well get an early night. Then came a sharp knock at the door. James had his own key and would simply have let himself in if he was returning earlier than planned.

She pulled her oversized cardigan more tightly around her body and padded down the corridor, placing an eye up to the spyhole, pausing for a fraction of a second before opening up.

Sergeant Sam Sharpe stood on the doorstep.

'Is there something wrong with your hotel?' Dani wanted to be jovial, but this nocturnal visit was most unwelcome.

'No, it's great, actually. There's been a development, can I come inside?'

Dani took a step back, sighing with resignation as she allowed the American to brush past her into the flat.

Chapter 12

He stood squarely in the middle of the kitchen, not making any move to take off his dark blue jacket.

Dani slowly took in Sam's appearance. The jacket was smart and although he wasn't wearing a tie, she could tell that the open-necked shirt was an expensive one. 'It looks like you've been somewhere special?'

'I've been at the Royal Concert Hall. But the evening was a blow-out.'

The DCI crinkled her brow.

'When I gave Vicki Kendrick my card the other day, it had my cell number on the back. She called me up yesterday afternoon.'

Dani frowned even further, wondering why she was only just hearing about this.

'Vicki said she wanted to talk more about Dale. She said that the shock of hearing about his death made her clam up when we were in her office.' Sam cleared his throat. 'She invited me to a recital she was giving this evening. Tickets were put aside for me at the door. The plan was to talk afterwards, over dinner.'

Dani wasn't sure why she felt so uncomfortable about this arrangement. Sam Sharpe was perfectly entitled to go on a date with whomever he chose. He might even have got more information out of the woman this way. 'Go on.'

'The gal was a no-show. We sat in that auditorium for a good forty five minutes before an embarrassed theatre manager came out to tell us the recital was cancelled, 'due to a last minute illness,' he said.'

'Okay, so Vicki's been taken ill. I don't quite see what that's got to do with me at ten o'clock in the evening.' Dani hadn't intended to sound so cranky.

'I've tried calling her dozens of times and there's no reply – either on her cell or home number. If I were back in Richmond I'd head over there and check things out. But I've no jurisdiction in Scotland.'

The words hung in the air for a few moments.

'You want me to send a squad car round to check she's alright?'

Sam shook his head steadily, finally starting to appear pissed off. '*No*, I want the both of us to go round there and check she's alright. Her brother was murdered less than a week ago. I think I've got a duty to make sure that the woman is safe.'

Dani disappeared into the bedroom, returning moments later having pulled on a pair of jeans instead of her jogging pants. 'I think you're over reacting, but it won't hurt to take a look.'

Sam threw his arms in the air. 'Well, thank you Ma'am.'

*

'What's Vicki's personal history?' Dani asked, as she drove them towards the west side of the city.

'According to her Wiki page, she was married to a fellow musician called Guy Kendrick for fifteen years. They divorced in 2010. There was no mention of anyone else,' Sam replied.

Dani swept her little car into an attractive terrace, where a neat row of Georgian homes formed a crescent ahead of them. The detectives got out and approached one of the grand front doors.

'This is the one,' Sam commented, pressing hard on the bell.

Dani tried to peer through the ground floor window but the shutters were closed. The place was in darkness.

'No response,' Sam called over.

'Is there a back entrance to this terrace?' Dani thought out loud.

'Let's go see,' Sam responded.

'Hang on,' Dani added, swiftly pulling out her warrant card. 'This is a nice area and Vicki is a sensible middle aged woman who lives alone.' The DCI stepped over a low wall and hammered the next-door-neighbour's knocker.

An elderly man opened up a crack, with chains still attached at top and bottom.

Dani held her identity card up close to him. 'My name is DCI Bevan from the Police Scotland Serious Crime Division. We've not been able to get hold of Ms Kendrick at number 25 this evening. Have you seen her at all?'

'I believe that my wife has.' The man's face disappeared, rapidly replaced by the suspicious eyes of an equally elderly lady.

'Vicki came home at around 4pm. We parked up at the same time. She said there was an important recital this evening. You'll find her at the Concert Hall in town.'

'She never turned up,' Dani replied gravely.

The eyes flickered to and fro. 'That's very unlike her. Vicki is the consummate professional.' The face disappeared once again, to be replaced by a bony hand, shoved through the gap between the door and the frame, with a Yale key gripped in its long fingers. 'You'd better have this Detective Inspector. Vicki may have been taken ill.'

Dani nodded her gratitude and took the key.

Sam stepped out of the shadows to join her. 'How very British. At least it wasn't sitting under a flower pot.'

'Oh, people do that too, don't you worry. It would have been the next place I'd have looked.'

Dani fitted the key into the lock and pushed her way inside. The hallway was wide and in total darkness.

'Ms Kendrick!' Sam called out. 'It's Sergeant Sharpe and DCI Bevan. We've come to check you're okay!'

There was no response.

Dani pulled the sleeves of her sweatshirt down to cover her hands, turning to Sam. 'Ever get the feeling you've stepped into a crime scene?'

'Yeah,' he muttered distractedly. 'Best not to touch anything we don't have to.'

Dani took a couple of long strides towards the sitting room door. She'd been to enough scenes of violent crime in her career to recognise the eerie stillness and the faintly metallic scent of death. There wasn't an opportunity to reach the room, however, as with her last step, Dani's foot slid unceremoniously in what felt like a deep pool of liquid on the floor. Her head struck the stone tiles as she fell. The DCI recalled no more after that except blackness.

Chapter 13

When Dani came to, she was lying on a sofa in a large kitchen-diner and could hear police sirens outside.

A sudden gust of cold air blasted her legs before a pair of paramedics rushed to her side. Dani glanced down then and saw the blood, which was streaked along the side of her jeans and sweater. It took the detective a couple of seconds to realise it wasn't hers.

'I'm fine,' she said shakily.

'How long were you unconscious?'

'A few minutes perhaps, I don't know for sure.'

'Then you'll need to come with us.'

'What about the blood? What's happened to Ms Kendrick?' Dani tried to sit up but her temples throbbed like crazy.

The paramedic shook his head. 'You're a detective, right?'

Dani nodded.

'Let's just say that she doesn't need *our* help any longer. Your people are taking it from here.'

*

It seemed like hours before Sam came into her room at the hospital.

'What the hell's going on?' She demanded. 'They won't let me out of this ruddy place.'

Sam looked pale. He sat on the edge of the bed. 'How are you feeling? I shouldn't have let you go on ahead in the dark. The perp could still have been in the building.'

'It's fine. I am trained for this kind of thing. What about Vicki? I'm taking it she's dead?'

'Yeah, and it was nasty. Her body was strung up from the light fitting, not far from the entrance to the sitting room, hence the blood on the floor. Vicki had multiple stab wounds to the neck and torso. It wasn't quick *or* painless. The doc reckoned she bled out.'

'Who attended the callout?'

'Phil and a young gal called Alice. She seemed very on-the-ball. And Phil was great. He didn't waste any time assuming I was the killer, who'd incapacitated you with a blow to the head and then taken the time to call the cops.'

'DI Boag is a sensible guy. He knows you.' He must also have wondered what the hell Sam was doing here in Glasgow with his boss, Dani imagined, even if he didn't ask.

'Don't worry, I explained everything, including the details of Dale's murder back in Richmond and his connection to Vicki. I told them you were helping me out as a friend – nothing official.'

'Well, it's going to be official now.'

Sam creased his face. 'There was no sign of a break-in and not much in the way of evidence indicating a struggle either. In fact, there were two glasses in the kitchen sink and a half finished bottle of wine on a counter.

'We might get prints?' Dani sat bolt upright, only to groan in discomfort.

'The place was wiped clean, according to the scene of crime techs. But at least we can be certain that Vicki knew this guy reasonably well. She must have let him in.'

'Then someone will have spotted the bastard. Those houses are close together. There must be plenty of comings and goings along that crescent in the early evening. Any news on the time of death?'

'Nothing official, but the doc suggested she'd been dead about three or four hours which fits with the murder taking place after she got home from the college and before setting out to the recital.'

Dani rested her hands in her lap, feeling the unpleasant sensation of dried blood on her trousers. The DCI sensed bile rise into her throat. 'Why has this happened now, Sam? We'd only just informed the poor woman that her brother had been murdered in cold blood and now this?'

Sam's expression was grim. 'There has to be a connection to the hit on Dale. The thing that's really bugging me about the timing, is the possibility that *I* was the one who led the killer right to her.'

Chapter 14

The new meeting room in the Glasgow Serious Crime Department was packed full. DCI Bevan was addressing her team from the front, but DCS Douglas was standing, menacingly, just a couple of inches to one side.

'We are now officially working with our colleagues in the Virginia PD, like we did in the Gordon Parker investigation a few years ago.'

Several heads nodded in recognition. The ones who remained impassive were newer to the division, including DS Alice Mann.

'Our link man is Sergeant Sam Sharpe.'

The American raised a hand to his forehead and gave a salute.

'He was looking into the death of Detective Dale Faulkner back in Richmond when his inquiries brought him to Scotland. Our previous working relationship encouraged him to share his findings with me, which at that stage were purely speculative.'

'But now Faulkner's sister has been murdered, it looks like more of a concrete connection,' Calder added.

'Do we know any more about the family?' Phil enquired.

Dani nodded, turning to a set of photographs pinned to the board behind her. 'Vicki Faulkner went to live with her grandmother, Maeve Lomas, at her council home in the Muirhouse estate in 1976, when her parents relocated to the US. Lomas died eight years ago of lymphatic cancer.'

Sam stood up and moved across to join the DCI.

'Dale's parents both died around a decade back. There was nothing suspicious about their deaths either. We're still looking into the existence of wider members of the Lomas and Faulkner families. It's certain that the Richmond branch pretty much lost contact with their Scottish relatives. I'm not sure that line of inquiry will bring us much further forward.'

'How did you make the Scottish connection in the first place?' DCS Douglas eyed the American detective with thinly veiled scepticism.

Sam prodded the white board with a beefy finger. 'It was these two names that brought me across the pond. Dale was shot in a derelict house on the Southside of Richmond. Its most recent tenants were a couple named McNeil. They had no kids and were teachers. It turns out that John McNeil's family hailed from Portencross West Kilbride, less than five miles from Dale's parents' farm, which they rented until the move to the States.'

'Have you interviewed this couple?'

Sam shook his head solemnly. 'Nobody's heard anything from them since 2014. That's when John and Rita gave up the lease on the house in Richmond. They could be anywhere by now.'

Douglas's expression stiffened. 'We've not got much to go on then, as far as the brother's shooting is concerned. I say we focus on Vicki Kendrick instead. It turns out the new DCC was a great fan of her playing.' The senior detective rolled his eyes.

Andy had to stop himself from letting out a laugh. Who knew that 'Dour' Douglas had a sense of humour?

'Of course sir,' Dani put in. 'Ms Kendrick's murder was right on our patch and it was a grisly one. Our investigation needs to begin with the forensics. Vicki let her murderer into the house, she even socialised with them. This person must have been acting normally for at least part of the evening. There have got to be traces of the perp somewhere on the premises.'

'Well, let me know when the PM results arrive. I'll need to keep the media informed of developments.' With that, the DCS swept from the room.

*

'Do we think the bastard was her lover?'

The discussion was flowing more freely now that Douglas had left.

'We've got to keep an open mind on that,' Dani replied.

'But to be able to string Kendrick up onto that light fitting, whilst she was still alive, must indicate a strong physical build, so we're surely assuming the killer was male?' DS Mann asserted.

'She asked me out pretty quick off the mark. I mean, I know Vicki wanted to find out more about Dale an' all, but I still got the distinct impression it was a date she was proposing.' Sam shifted awkwardly from one foot to the other.

'Which tells us nothing,' DC Clifton supplied. 'The woman was a long term divorcee and free to see any man she wished. Just because she asked out Sergeant Sharpe, it doesn't mean she didn't have other boyfriends.'

'Aye, Dan's quite right,' Andy continued. 'But her coming onto Sam suggests the woman was sexually active. That means men could've come back to her house reasonably often, which makes our job a hell of a lot more difficult.'

'Hopefully, the house-to-house inquiries should shed some light on that.' Dani sighed. 'But I take your point. If Vicki had a long-term partner with whom she was monogamous, it would provide us with an immediate suspect.'

Phil stood up. 'But if Kendrick was killed by the same people who shot her brother, then we should be setting out on quite a different track altogether.'

Dani was quiet for a moment, putting a hand absent-mindedly to the ugly purple bump on the side of her head. 'Phil's right. We need to split this investigation into two. Sam and Andy can look into the Richmond connection whilst the rest of the team focus purely on Kendrick and her lovers.'

Sam crinkled his brow. 'Don't I get any more manpower than that?'

'If your investigation turns something up, I'll reassess. In the meantime, I trust you two to do an excellent job.'

Andy Calder slapped the American on the back playfully. 'Looks like you're stuck wi' me, pal!' he declared, a wide grin on his handsome face.

Chapter 15

A tiny estate of grey-clad new-build houses stretched out before them. The land in this small valley was gently undulating and featureless but close enough to the coast to be battered by merciless winds.

'So the farm no longer exists?' Sam stood next to the car and glanced about him.

'The owner sold off the land that Crosbie Farm stood on twenty odd years back. Since then, there's only been some light manufacturing in the area. The planning department of the council told me this estate was only put up in the last eighteen months. They're adding new houses all the time, when the demand arises.'

'We're not going to find out much by hanging around here then.' Sam sighed, sensing the enormity of the task.

Andy laid an Ordnance Survey map out on the roof, its corners flapping madly in the breeze. 'There's a hotel up at the point, near Portencross Castle. I thought we could start by asking a few questions of the manager?'

Sam shrugged his broad shoulders. 'Sure, you lead the way.' For some reason, the American wasn't keen to remain in this spot. It was isolated and possessed no redeeming features that he could identify.

The DS folded up the pages and climbed back into the driving seat, performing a U-turn which took them out of the estate by the quickest possible route.

*

Sergeant Sharpe found Portencross far more appealing. A wide expanse of sandy beach was overlooked by a well preserved stone castle, positioned on a stony promontory which faced out towards the Firth of Clyde and with a set of impressive mountains visible in the distance.

'What's over the water?' Sam asked his companion, as they headed towards an equally fortress-like hotel at the top of the beach.

'It's the hills of Arran. If you've not been there yet, you really should. It's like a little piece of heaven on Glesga's doorstep.'

Sam was happy to take Andy's word for this. He knew that Calder's approbation wasn't easily earned.

They approached the front of the hotel and sensed its function was more as a public house than anything else. The men pushed through a set of heavy wooden doors and approached the bar.

Andy brought out his warrant card and displayed it to the middle aged woman who was serving. 'We'll have a couple of pints of coke and take a look at your lunch menu, darlin'. But after that we'd like a word with the manager.'

The woman dispensed the cokes and pushed a pair of dog-eared menus in their direction. 'Aye, I'll send Rob over with your orders. You can have a word then.'

Sam carried the drinks to a table by a set of tall windows, offering up an impressive view. He'd been persuaded to have something called a Scotch pie, which Andy said would fuel them up against the chill.

The manager, Rob Shepherd, brought over their plates of pies and beans, perching on a stool to join them while they ate. 'Sal says your wantin' a word. Detectives from Glesga, is that right?'

'Aye,' Andy replied. 'But my colleague here is from America. He's investigating the death of a man who grew up in this area.'

Sam brought a photograph of Dale Faulkner out of his jacket pocket. 'He spent the first eight years of his life with his family at Crosbie Farm, where that new housing estate has been built. The parents were called Magnus and Susan Faulkner.'

Rob narrowed his eyes. 'I wouldn't have recognised him as an adult. He looks really muscly and bulked up. When Dale was a lad he was a scrawny wee devil.'

'You knew him?' Sam was immediately alert.

'We were at school together. Well, I'm a few years older than him. It was Vicki who was in my class. But it was a small village primary. We pretty much knew everyone.' Rob took the snapshot from the American's hand and examined it more closely. 'Do you say he's dead? That's a real shame.'

'Dale became a detective in my department in Richmond, Virginia. He was killed during a routine call out a couple of weeks back.' Sam shifted in his seat. 'Have you seen the news over the last few days?'

Rob's expression was cautious. 'Should I have done?'

'A woman was murdered the other evening in her Glasgow home, Mr Shepherd. She was known as Vicki Kendrick, maiden name Faulkner,' Andy explained.

The manager dropped the picture as if it were suddenly on fire. 'Jeez, was that *Vicki Faulkner*? I had no idea. And Dale killed too?' He appeared genuinely confused and upset.

'What can you tell us about the family? There seems hardly anyone left to ask.' Andy shifted forward, shovelling beans into his mouth to allow the man to talk.

'My parents ran the hotel here before I did. They took some of their supplies from the Faulkners up at Crosbie Farm – eggs, milk, that kind of thing. I remember one winter very well. It was during the seventies and the workers were all out on strike. My Da' always said it was the best business he ever did. Whenever the power went out, folk came in here to the pub where we had the log fires burning and we had our own generator out back. The alcohol helped too.'

Sam chuckled. 'What year would that have been, sir?'

'1974 was the era of the three-day week. Do you think that's when it might have been?' Andy offered.

Rob nodded. 'Aye, that would have made me about ten years old, which certainly fits. Anyways, we saw a lot of the Faulkners that year because there were shortages of all kinds of goods in the shops. So folk went direct to the local farms and bought food. It was like going back to the war, I suppose, although I'm too young to remember that! It made my parents pals with the Faulkners; brought the whole community together, in fact.'

'It was two years after that when Dale's Mom and Dad sold up and shipped out to the States. Do you know why they made such a big move?'

'We were very surprised,' Rob said. 'It was something that Magnus would have been up for, I'm sure, but the mum, Sue, was a quiet woman. I expect she was persuaded to go along with it. Magnus probably hoped to make his fortune out there.'

'What did you think of the fact that Vicki stayed behind with her Gran? Did your parents ever comment on it?' Andy watched his face closely.

Rob frowned. 'How do you mean?'

'Vicki never went to Richmond with her folks,' Sam continued. 'She was about to start at a decent school in the city where she was given a music scholarship. The girl lived with her maternal grandmother in Glasgow.'

Rob was wide-eyed. 'Well, I'll be damned. I suppose we simply assumed the girl had gone to America with her folks. But the Faulkners never told us otherwise. My parents had no idea Vicki remained in Scotland, I'd swear to that. Otherwise, they'd have kept in touch with her, had her back here in Portencross to stay.'

Sam observed the man's body language, he was hugging his arms across his chest and the American was sure he could see Rob's eyes glistening.

'I'm sorry, this news has come as a shock. It's bad enough to discover the kids are both dead, but to know that Vicki was just up the road from here all those years and Magnus and Sue left her behind. Well, it's simply heart-breaking.'

Chapter 16

'All the neighbours have been questioned, Ma'am.' Alice Mann took the chair in front of Dani's desk. 'The interiors are designed so that most of the living goes on at the rear, facing the communal gardens and the Kelvingrove Park beyond.'

'So nobody saw a damned thing?'

Alice shook her head. 'Certainly not the murderer being let in through Vicki's front door.'

'Could the perp have come in through the back? If this was a lover that the victim wanted to keep quiet, she may have instructed him to avoid entering from the street.'

'That's a definite possibility. The houses are designed with a footpath running along the rear of the terrace. There are gates leading off it that give access to the gardens. If the killer knew the layout, they'd be aware of this. The path is obscured by a tall hedge. It would have been very difficult for them to be seen by residents.'

'Like a little rat run,' Dani commented with a sigh. 'How about regular visitors to Kendrick's place, any comments on that?'

'The neighbours who provided you with the key seemed to know the victim best. They were very surprised at the suggestion she may have had more than one male visitor. Apparently, Vicki has been single since the divorce and appeared content being so. But the woman had plenty of friends at the college and fellow musicians who attended dinner parties at the house.'

'Could they provide any names?'

Alice shook her head. 'No, not really. But I'm

hoping to find out more from her colleagues at the college and her booking agent. She'd been with him for fifteen years. Vicki's mobile phone records didn't throw up anything out of the ordinary. Most of the calls were to her agent and concert hall venues, that kind of thing. Dan will be interviewing the ex-husband today, although Vicki hadn't had contact with him for a while, judging by her call history.'

'Yes, but he may be able to fill in some of the gaps we have in Vicki's past. Excellent work, Alice. You've been very thorough. The PM results came back this morning. I'll send them on to you. Vicki died as a result of multiple stab wounds, one to the neck which severed the carotid artery and caused her to lose a catastrophic amount of blood. It took forty five minutes for her to lose consciousness. She hadn't eaten since lunchtime but had drunk close to half a bottle of red wine in the previous couple of hours. In fact, the doc suggested that the condition of her liver indicated she was a regular, heavy drinker.'

'Does he think she was an alcoholic?'

'I don't believe so. He simply pointed out that she drank every day and had done for some considerable time. She had a very slight frame. The alcohol had done more damage than it would if that were not the case. I expect she knew her limits though, Vicki wouldn't have been able to perform her recitals otherwise.'

'The drinking could have started after the divorce, perhaps?'

'Possibly, or maybe it'd been going on even longer than that. I sensed when we met her, that Ms Kendrick wasn't a very happy woman.'

As the DS stood up to leave, Dani cleared her throat.

'Was there anything else, Ma'am?'

'What angle is DI Boag working on?' Dani made the request sound casual.

'He is researching Kendrick's family history – looking into the grandmother's background and Vicki's schooling. He's trying to find if there was any contact between them and the Faulkners in the USA after '76.'

The DCI visibly relaxed. 'Just the right job for Phil. It's the kind of stuff he's best at.'

'Yes, that's what we decided.' Alice made a move for the door again. 'Will that be all, Ma'am?'

'Certainly.' She managed an encouraging smile. 'But keep me updated on any developments.'

*

DC Dan Clifton pressed on the buzzer for the loft apartment situated on a narrow alley just off Cathedral Street. The front door gave a click and Dan pushed it open. He jogged up a couple of flights and found a middle aged man, tall and of medium build, with a full, grey tinged beard waiting for him on the landing.

'Detective Constable Clifton?'

'Aye.' Dan got out his warrant card, embarrassed to be slightly out of breath.

'I'm Guy Kendrick, do come inside, and please excuse the mess. My girlfriend is in the middle of an exhibition. Her artwork is everywhere.'

Dan followed the man into a cavernous, open-plan apartment. There were several large, colourful canvases propped up around the lounge area, but other than that, the detective would have said the place was very neat and tidy.

'I've just made coffee. Do you want to join me for a cup?' Guy slipped behind a kitchen counter and began bringing mugs down from a shelf.

If the DC didn't know any better, he would have made the flip judgement that Kendrick was gay. There was something about his manner that created this impression. After all, it took one to know one, Dan always thought. But then, the man was an artsy type, which sometimes made it difficult to tell.

'Any news on Vic's funeral? Will you be releasing her body anytime soon?'

'Oh, not yet sir. It's a murder investigation. There will be no funeral until all the forensic work has been completed.'

Kendrick perched on a stool and pushed a cup of coffee towards Dan. 'It's absolutely tragic. I wasn't aware of Vic having anyone special on the scene right now, so I'd be happy to organise some kind of send-off for her. She'd no family alive any longer. Unless Ken is going to take charge of her affairs.'

'Ken?' Dan fished out his notebook.

'Kenneth Rachmann, Vic's agent. He did everything for her. She relied very heavily on him, especially after we split.'

'But relations remained good between you and Ms Kendrick?'

'Well, they have been in the last few years. When we first separated it was a different story. You don't end a fifteen year marriage unless things are pretty bad between you.'

'Can I ask what caused the divorce?' Dan cleared his throat, uncomfortable to be asking these questions but knowing they were crucial to the investigation. This was the type of thing he sensed Alice would take in her stride.

Kendrick sipped his drink. 'I could say we'd simply drifted apart, but that would only be half of the story. The truth is that I had an affair when I was on tour in the summer of 2009. I play classical guitar and was a member of the orchestra attached to a popular show that season.'

'Did Vicki find out about it?'

'I told her, after I returned in the autumn. We had an absolutely blazing row. The type you never forget as long as you live.'

'Was there violence involved?'

Kendrick smiled sadly. 'No, Detective. Vic was a small, delicate woman. I was always aware of my physical superiority. I never so much as raised a hand in anger towards her. Anyway, I was in the wrong. The ire was directed almost entirely at me.'

'Would it be accurate to say that you left Vicki for another woman?'

'No, because it was just a fling.' Kendrick put down his cup. 'Are you married?'

'No, I'm not.'

'Because my marriage to Vicki wasn't conventional. We were both professional musicians and made our living by touring the globe. We spent many months apart from one another. It works in the beginning, when the buzz of the reunions maintains excitement in the relationship. Then one or other of you starts to want more - a stable, day-to-day kind of set-up. That person was me. Vic enjoyed the itinerant lifestyle. Let's face it, she was a lot more successful at the whole thing than I was.'

'There were no children?'

He shook his head. 'Vic never wanted them. She'd been orphaned young and was brought up by her grandmother. She always claimed she didn't have a clue how a family worked and would be useless at it.'

Dan frowned. 'I'm afraid that wasn't entirely true.'

'How do you mean?' Kendrick's posture stiffened.

'Vicki's parents only died ten years ago. They

moved to the United States with her younger brother in 1976 and Vicki stayed with her gran in Glasgow. She may never have had contact with them, but they certainly weren't dead.'

The man rose from his seat, his face ashen. 'But she told me all the details – about the car accident that killed them. I met her grandmother on several occasions. I believe we even talked about it together once.'

'Perhaps you should sit down again, sir. Have you got any brandy in the flat?'

Kendrick nodded, gesturing towards a wooden sideboard. He fell back onto the stool, gripping the worktop with both hands. 'I don't know why, but I find that news more shocking than when the police told me she was dead.'

Dan carried the bottle across the room and put a generous dash in his host's empty cup.

Kendrick knocked it back in a single arm action. 'Why would Vic have lied about something like that? And about having a brother as well? Jesus, this is too much to comprehend.'

'Her brother is also deceased, but only recently. So you have no recollection of Vicki making contact with her American family during the years you were married?'

'I never knew they existed for Christ's sake!' Kendrick turned to look Dan in the eye. 'Vic toured the States a great deal, especially during the nineties. I suppose she must have hooked up with her family then, even if she never told me about it.'

'We have no evidence to suggest that. According to your ex-wife before she died, the last time she set eyes on them was when they left for Virginia in 1976.'

Kendrick reached for the bottle and poured another generous measure. He dipped his head towards Dan. 'Do you want some?'

'No thanks.'

'This is the weirdest shit I've ever heard. I lived with Vic for fifteen years. We were close during that time, far closer than I am to my current girlfriend. But she kept this secret from me – worse than that, she constructed an elaborate lie about her past.'

'Is there anyone she may have told the truth to?'

Kendrick narrowed his eyes, which were beginning to become unfocussed. 'Vic didn't have many friends. She travelled too much. The only constant in her life was her grandmother. Then, when Maeve passed away it was me and Ken.'

'So her agent might know more about Vicki's past?'

'It's possible, I suppose. But to be perfectly frank with you, if Vic didn't tell me all this stuff when we were first together, totally in love and opening up about everything, then I don't believe she ever shared it with another living soul.'

Chapter 17

The tail end of some kind of trans-Atlantic storm was whipping up the Clyde that evening, splattering rain onto the windows of The Castle Hotel, as if a person was standing outside with a bucket, creating a scene for a low-budget horror movie.

Sam and Andy had decided to book rooms there for the night, after a day of asking questions around the shops and farms of Portencross and Seamill. The detectives ended their labours seated by one of the open fires, a couple of peat dark single malts on the table between them. The place was empty apart from a group of seasoned golfers congregated around the bar.

A handful of locals had recalled the Faulkners when they worked Crosbie Farm back in the seventies, but none gave them as much information as Rob Shepherd had.

Sam took a swig of his dram. 'Damn, that's seriously good stuff. Almost worth the weather.'

'Steady on, that's fightin' talk,' Andy rumbled, before cracking a grin. 'Aye, it's fair dreich out there the' nicht.'

'I'm not sure what you just said, but I think I'm in total agreement.'

Andy laughed.

Sam's expression became more serious. 'So, Dani's happy with this James guy?'

'I have to admit that she is. I wasn't sure about him at first, but he's grown on me.'

'Yeah, I can tell she's more grounded.'

'To be honest, the boss was a mess when youse two were together. We had that case in Norway and it played around with her head. It was just a shame that it was you she was with when all that stuff with her mother kicked off as well.'

Sam shuffled forward. 'Yeah, speaking of the Norway investigation, I always thought something went on with Dani on that trip. She was different when she came back. Can you shed any light on that for me?'

Andy put the whisky glass to his lips, hoping he might be able to side-step the question. Then he found he didn't have to. The door to the public bar flew open. At first, the DC thought it may have been dislodged by the wind. He soon realised there was a more human cause.

A huge man in a black raincoat stood on the threshold. It quickly became evident that it was one of his substantial boots which had forced the door practically off its hinges.

Rob lifted the hatch and walked round the bar to face him. 'I don't want any trouble Mac.'

'I've no argument wi' you or your missus. But I hear that a couple of polis have been asking after the Faulkners. A wee bird tells me they've wound up here.'

'Just a few routine inquiries, I think.' Rob kept his tone neutral.

Mac's hooded eyes took in the room. 'Is that them o'er there by the fire?'

Rob shrugged noncommittally.

Sam decided it was time to intervene. He stood up. 'I'm Sergeant Sam Sharpe. This is my colleague DS Calder. We've been the ones asking the questions. Is there a problem with that?'

Mac was lighter on his feet than he looked. Within seconds, he'd moved in on Sam, grabbing his lapels and placing his face so close to the American's that their noses were practically touching. 'The problem pal, is that I've been looking for that scumbag family for the best part of four decades, so if you know what rock they're all hiding under, you'd better tell me noo, or I'll knock those perfect yankee teeth doon the back of yer throat.'

It didn't take long for Andy to sweep Mac's arm behind his back and lodge a knee firmly into the base of his spine. The man winced with pain.

Sam took a good look at his heavily lined face. It was clear that Mac was at least sixty years old and not as strong as he thought he was. 'Now, if you promise to behave, my friend will let you sit on that stool there and have a little chat with us. If not, we'll drag you down to the jailhouse in Seamill for the night. What do you say?'

'Just let go of my arm for Christ's sake,' he whined pitifully.

Andy manoeuvred his captive onto a stool and released his grip, just a fraction.

Rob came over with another glass of whisky. 'He'll be fine after he's drunk this. Mac's harmless enough.'

Sam brushed down his shirt, not sure he was inclined to agree.

Andy took the seat beside the big man, making certain he could quickly restrain him again if necessary.

'Now, Mac is it? Just why have you been searching for the Faulkners all these years?' Sam looked him up and down. The man was old, but had clearly at one time in his life been a serious piece of muscle.

Mac downed the drink before answering. 'I had unfinished business wi' Magnus, that's all.'

'What kind of business?'

'He owed me money. When I went up to the farmhouse to get it off him they'd all gone. The place was cleared out. They didn't ever come back.'

Andy wasn't surprised, with a younger and fitter Mac lying in wait for them here in Portencross.

'And you're sure *you* never tracked them down?' Sam watched Mac's expression carefully. 'You would have been real mad after all these years when you finally got hold of a member of the Faulkner family.'

Mac whipped his head up. 'Did they go to *America*? Is that why there's a yankee detective here askin' questions about them?' His thick legs began twitching ferociously.

Andy was genuinely concerned he might have to fight the man again. 'They're all dead, pal. You won't be getting your money now, even if you do find out where they took off to back then.'

Mac banged a fist down hard on the table, sending the empty glasses a couple of inches into the air. 'Those thieving bastards got away wi' ma money!'

Sam sat back against the bench and said nothing. He simply marvelled at the terrible, tragic irony of the man's words.

Chapter 18

Vicki Kendrick's agent, Kenneth Rachmann, ran his business from a suite of offices on Baird Street, not far from the college where his client had taught music.

DS Mann had made an appointment and was expected. A middle aged secretary made the detective a cup of tea whilst she waited in a seating area. It didn't take long for Rachmann to open the door to his office and invite her in.

Alice brought her mug along too. 'My name is Detective Sergeant Mann. We spoke earlier.'

'Do take a seat, Sergeant. I see Maggie has already furnished you with a drink. She's very good that way.' The man made himself comfortable in a large leather chair. He was diminutive in stature and almost entirely bald.

Alice struggled to imagine him capable of overpowering Ms Kendrick, although Dan had told her that the ex-husband would have be more than capable of doing so. 'I need to ask you a few questions about Vicki Kendrick, I'm afraid. Had you worked together long?'

'Vicki approached my agency in 2001. I took on her representation a couple of months after that. I've had clients for longer, but I considered Vicki a dear friend.'

'I'm sorry for your loss, sir. When did you last speak with her?'

'It was on Saturday morning. I called to remind her about the recital at the Concert Hall on the Thursday evening and to discuss a tour we had planned for Canada in the summer.' Rachmann sighed heavily. 'Of course, the dates will all have to be cancelled now and the relevant people informed. Her fans will be deeply upset by the news.'

'How did Vicki seem when you spoke – what was her mood like?'

'She was very upbeat. It felt as if I'd interrupted her as she was about to go out of the door as a matter of fact. The conversation was brief but pleasant. I believe she was looking forward to the Canadian trip particularly. Vicki has good friends out there.' He rubbed his hairless chin. 'I wonder if they've been informed yet. Perhaps I should do it.'

'I expect it will be on all the news bulletins by this evening. The international press will get hold of the story soon enough,' Alice replied brusquely.

Rachmann felt the policewoman had missed his point slightly. 'Has Guy been told?'

'Yes, Mr Kendrick has already been interviewed. He thought you might have more insight into Vicki's social life in the weeks leading up to her death than he did.'

The man shrugged his shoulders. 'Vicki was a private woman. She was very well known in the classical music world. Her television appearances in recent years had made her recognisable to the general public too. She preferred to frequent the bars and restaurants in the cities we toured rather than her native Glasgow. It was more anonymous that way.'

'Did Vicki have a boyfriend?'

'To my knowledge, she did not. Since her divorce there were a handful of discreet romances but nothing serious and nobody within the last year.'

'I'll need you to provide me with the names of these men, please.'

'Of course, in the cases where I can recall them. A couple were rather casual.'

'Yet Ms Kendrick still told you about the affairs?'

'We were friends and spoke about everything. My life was an open book to Vicki. After my wife died I went through a very trying time. She was my confidante.'

'I will need to look at Vicki's diaries for the last five years. We'll need to see the records of where she performed and who with.'

'Yes, I can do that with ease. The information is all computerized.'

Alice looked up from her notes. 'What did you know about Vicki's background?'

Rachmann's expression became guarded. 'Vicki was a private person, I told you that. I knew her grandmother before she died. Other than Guy, that's the only family of hers I've ever met.'

'Did she tell you what happened to her parents?'

He sighed deeply. 'I suppose you already know about it so there's no point in being cryptic. Her parents moved to America in the 70s and Vicki remained in Scotland. They lost touch and I think Vic was ashamed about the situation, so she told people they were dead.'

'Even her own husband of fifteen years? Didn't you think that was odd? Why did she tell you the truth and not him?'

'I suppose that somewhere in her heart she never fully trusted Guy. It turned out that her instinct was accurate. I don't know why she chose to share the truth with me but I'm honoured she did so.'

'I will need to get you to make a statement accounting for your movements on the evening Vicki was killed. We require it of everyone who knew her.'

'Of course. I'll get Maggie to type it up for us.' Rachmann leant forward. 'Although Vic told me the truth about her family, I always sensed there was more. The woman had many secrets, I'm certain of that. I really hope it wasn't one of those secrets that got her murdered, not when she could have come to me for help. But Vicki thought she was completely alone in this world, Detective Sergeant, perhaps in a way that only those who've learnt to live without their close family can ever hope to comprehend.'

Alice nodded, feeling she was beginning to understand the strange way that Vicki Kendrick had lived her life.

Chapter 19

The fierce gales and torrential rain of the previous night had subsided. Sam stood at the window of his room and gazed out across the Firth at the impressive view, a cup of instant coffee from the refreshment tray cradled in his hands.

It turned out that 'Mac' was Ciaran McAlister, a long term resident of Portencross, who once owned the shop and garage on the A78, just past the town of Seamill. Rob Shepherd was required to drive the man home to his flat after the bar closed. He was in far too much of an emotional state to have managed the walk alone.

Sam didn't seriously believe that McAlister could have organised the hit on Dale or murdered Vicki in her Glasgow home. But the fact remained, he was the only person they'd come across so far who actually had a motive to do so.

There was a knock at the door.

'Come in, it's open!'

Andy entered with his own mug of tea. 'I've brought bourbon biscuits for breakfast.' He tossed a mini pack of three on the bed, glancing across at the window. 'Ah, I see you're the one with the view.'

'I suppose Rob thought I was the closest he had to a proper tourist.'

'Not a problem. I know that landscape well enough.'

Sam bent down to retrieve a biscuit from the packet. He examined it closely. 'Is there actually bourbon in these?'

Andy laughed. 'Sadly not. I haven't got the slightest idea why they're called that. They taste great so I've never questioned it.'

Sam munched on the biscuit for a while. 'So when the Faulkners set out for Richmond they had unpaid debts here in Scotland. Do you think that's why they left?'

'It's very likely. Maybe they owed money to people even nastier than our friend Mac.'

Sam gazed out to sea. 'But why kill the children all these years later, if we're looking for a disgruntled creditor? I don't see what it could have achieved. Vicki Kendrick *had* got money, but the person who murdered her didn't take anything valuable from the house or force her to give them access to her bank account. Her savings and investments are intact.'

'The crime scene details seemed to suggest a frenzied and personal attack. You were there, what did you reckon?'

'The killing was brutal and merciless. Vicki was a small woman, unable to defend herself against such anger.' Sam turned back to look at his colleague.

'Is a forty year old bad debt left by her parents enough to explain the ferocity of that hatred?' Andy asked levelly.

'No,' the American said quietly. 'I don't believe it is.'

*

The McNeil family were well known in Seamill. They'd once owned the large Hydro Hotel and plenty of descendants of the clan were still scattered about the area.

Sam and Andy were waiting to meet one of them, in the lounge bar of the town's main hotel. He was a local historian called Ian McNeil, who Calder found through an internet search.

McNeil, broad and middle aged, approached their

table and put out his hand to the men. 'My name is Ian. I take it you're the police officers from Glasgow?'

'Are we that obvious?' Andy replied with a grin.

'At this time of the year you'd either be a golfer or visiting the hotel for a pensioners' lunch. You don't fit the bill on either score.'

They ordered morning coffee from a waitress in a fetching tartan outfit.

'How may I help you?' Ian placed his hands on the table and eyed both detectives.

'You wrote a book on the history of the McNeil clan, I believe?'

'Aye, it was published by a local operation five years back. It's not topped the bestseller lists yet but you'll find several copies in the village shop.'

'And you teach at the local school?'

'That's right, I'm Head of History at the High School in West Kilbride. Are you American? I thought you were both down from Glasgow?'

Sam smiled. 'I'm from Richmond, Virginia. A case involving a couple of your clansfolk has brought me over this way.'

Ian leant forward. 'Now, that *is* interesting. There is a chapter in my book dedicated to the McNeils in the USA, but my research was only very perfunctory in that area. It really deserves a book of its own and I'd need to travel out there to do proper justice to the topic.'

Sam slipped out his notebook and showed the man a page from it. 'This couple, John and Rita McNeil, claimed to have ancestors who hailed from Portencross, although they were both born and bred in the US. They taught school in downtown Richmond.'

Ian pulled on a pair of dark rimmed glasses and reached for a bag by his feet. 'I've brought along some documentation of my own.' He pushed aside the coffee cups and laid out a large and detailed family tree which had been rolled up inside a cardboard cylinder. 'These are the McNeils, going back to the early nineteenth century. I've got a tree at home which stretches back even further, but for our purposes, I thought this would do.'

'It will do very nicely, sir,' Sam muttered gratefully.

'What age would this John McNeil be now?'

Sam rubbed his stubbly chin. 'The tenancy details suggested he would be around sixty years old.'

Ian ran his finger down the divisions and subdivisions of the intricate document. 'A small branch of the McNeil family set sail to the United States in the 1840s. The men were headed out to make their fortune in the construction boom taking place in your great cities during that time.'

'Do you know if any of them ended up in Virginia?' Sam's interest had been piqued.

'As a matter of fact I have some information about that.' Ian sat back and folded his arms across his chest. 'I'm sure you're aware that Richmond was a Confederate stronghold during the Civil War.'

'I sure am.'

'In the 1860s, Richmond possessed the largest factory in the confederacy. It was called the Tredegar Iron Works. It turned out hundreds of tons of heavy ordnance machinery, artillery and other munitions. My ancestor, William McNeil, travelled to the city to find work there in 1862. He and his wife had two grown up sons then, both who fought in the Confederate army.'

'Do you think this may have been the branch of the family that John McNeil descended from?'

Ian leant forward again and pointed at the diagram. 'Here is William McNeil and his wife Mary.

One of their sons was killed in the Union campaign against the city in 1864 but the other, Samuel, survived the war and had three children. Your John McNeil must be the great grandson of Samuel's youngest boy, George William McNeil.'

Sam looked closely at the section of the tree Ian was indicating. 'Yes, I see. The birth dates seem to match. How did you get this information? Do you know anything more about John?'

Ian smiled sadly and shook his head. 'Everything I've got here originates from American online genealogy sites. The information comes from birth and death certificates, census reports, that kind of thing. I did find some books that had been written about the Tredegar Iron Works during the Civil War which gave me a little more context. But like I said before, I'd need to visit the States myself to come up with anything more substantial.'

Sam sighed, he wasn't sure if this knowledge actually took them any further forward. 'So all of this stuff is of public record? John McNeil would most likely have known about his family history and the connection to West Kilbride?'

'Oh yes, if he had an interest in his family's Scottish roots then it would have been straightforward for him to find out all of this for himself.'

'John McNeil told his classes that his family were Scottish and that his ancestral home was Portencross, West Kilbride. So this guy had clearly done some research into the family tree,' Andy clarified. 'Then Dale Faulkner, one time resident of Portencross, winds up dead in a house who's most recent tenants were the McNeils. How can that be a coincidence? What's the connection between them?'

'I don't know the details of your case,' Ian added, 'I can only speculate using my knowledge of how the typical genealogist works. Perhaps John McNeil came across Faulkner's name as part of his research into the McNeils of West Kilbride. The communities here are small and intertwined. This may have prompted him to contact the man. That's what I would do, if I wanted to add another name to my tree, or clarify a historical detail. I would get in touch with a living descendent.'

'But Dale didn't want anyone knowing about his past in Scotland,' Sam said quietly.

'That's very unusual for an American, if I might say. I find that your citizens are very keen to celebrate their Celtic heritage. John McNeil would certainly not have thought the subject was taboo, I should imagine.'

Sam placed a hand on the man's arm. 'You're quite right, Ian. But if John McNeil *had* approached Dale in Richmond about his past, my old friend sure wouldn't have been too happy about it.'

Andy nodded to the older man. 'Thanks for the input. This has been a really great help. And can we get some kind of copy of this?' He gestured towards the document laid out across the table.

'Of course, I've several at home. I might even throw in a signed copy of my book whilst I'm at it.'

Chapter 20

DI Phil Boag was leading their briefing with the results of his research into Vicki Kendrick's family.

'Magnus Faulkner married Susan Lomas in the summer of 1962. Vicki was born in '65 and Dale in '67. There were no living grandparents except for Susan's mother, Mauve Lomas, who died in 2008 at the age of 89. She'd been the guardian of Vicki since December 1976. They lived together on the Muirhouse estate until Vicki completed her schooling at The Monteith Academy for Girls. Then she studied at the College of Music and took digs in the city centre, where she has had her main home since the nineties.'

'It must have been tough, living in a tiny council flat on the Muirhouse whilst attending such a prestigious school,' Dani commented. 'Vicki must have come from a very different background to her peers.'

'She was a scholarship student,' Alice added. 'That's just what it's like when you get your fees waived because of a particular skill or talent. I suppose the child learns to see the situation as a fantastic opportunity rather than a burden.'

Dani immediately wondered if Alice were speaking from experience.

'Well, Vicki certainly took full advantage of that opportunity,' Phil continued. 'She was named Scottish Musician of the Year in 1995 and toured the world in '96 and '97.'

'What about other family members: uncles, aunts, cousins?' Dani counted them off on her fingers.

'There were a few cousins on the Lomas side, who lived in and around Glasgow. I spoke with one of them yesterday, a lady of a similar age to Vicki. She said they saw one another every so often when Vicki still lived with her gran, but when she became successful, they didn't hear a dickie bird. This cousin suggested she may not even attend the funeral.'

'What about the Faulkners?'

'Magnus had two brothers, Joe and Keith. The younger one died in the eighties and the older more recently, just a couple of years ago. He was in his late seventies. Neither had any children.'

'I suppose that if Vicki had cut off her own father, mother and brother so easily she was unlikely to have maintained a link to this particular uncle.' Dani sighed.

'There was certainly no evidence of it,' Phil replied.

'How are Sergeant Sharpe and DS Calder getting on in West Kilbride?' Alice asked.

'Apparently, the Faulkners owed money to at least one local heavy before they moved to Virginia. They never told their local friends that Vicki was staying behind either.'

'I expect they were worried she might get targeted by their creditors if they did,' Alice responded.

'I suppose that explains their decision to leave the country and begin a new life,' Phil concluded.

Dani turned to look at the evidence taped to the board. 'Yes, but I'm struggling to see how it connects to Vicki's murder. This crime wasn't a theft that went wrong. Nothing valuable was taken. It may have been a revenge attack but then why now? Would you really inflict all those blows to such a delicate, defenceless woman over some money owed by her parents forty years ago?'

'There has to be more to it,' Alice asserted. 'The grudge had to be more personal to Vicki and her brother. The forensic results suggest that this person wiped the place clean after the murder. There weren't even any footprints in the blood - other than yours, boss - which indicates an element of professionalism and pre-planning.'

'A cold and professional clean-up job, yet the murder itself was frenzied, using a knife from Vicki's own kitchen drawer.' Dani was silent for a moment. 'Could we be looking at two perps?'

'One who kills and another who mops up the mess, you mean?' Alice took a step closer to the board and stared hard at the scene of crime photos.

But Phil shook his head. 'It would have been difficult enough to get one person in and out of that house unnoticed, never mind two. The forensics would surely have indicated more activity if there were multiple attackers. I just don't buy it.'

Dani nodded. 'Yeah, I take your points Phil, but I want us to keep an open mind on this. For the time being, we need to focus on Vicki's social life in the last few weeks. Someone must have known about a new friend she was meeting, having dinner with, was comfortable enough to invite into her home for drinks. Get back to St Mungo's College and speak to anyone who even gave Vicki the time of day since she's worked there.' Dani turned to face the room. 'Let's keep digging. This bastard can't be the bloody invisible man.'

*

Dani had been summoned to meet with DCS Douglas in his office. She found the man surrounded by notes and files when she entered. The DCI immediately noted the contrast to her old boss, whose desk used to be as shiny and free of clutter as a minimalist sculpture at the Museum of Modern Art. But then Nicholson hadn't been much of a details man.

'Ah, Danielle, take a seat. What's the latest on the Kendrick case?'

'Forensics have drawn a blank, but we're hopeful about tracking down her lovers. We've already got several names. DS Mann has been extremely thorough.'

'Dour' Douglas narrowed his dark eyes. 'What about DI Boag – is he not so thorough in his work?'

'That's not what I meant at all. Phil has made good progress on Kendrick's background. It's the kind of stuff he excels at.'

Douglas tapped his pen on the desk. 'But not on the fieldwork, witness interviews, scene examination etcetera?'

It was a leading question. Dani wasn't keen to answer it. 'Phil was behind a desk for a long time. He isn't the best officer I have on those areas just yet, but I'm working on it. If he's a bit rusty in the field then that's my responsibility.'

'Only I've had a complaint.' Douglas put the pen down and folded his arms.

'Oh, I see.' She wondered who the bloody hell from.

'Not against Phil. The complaint was made by the CEO of Hemingway Shipyards to the new DCC. Apparently, DS Calder made a nuisance of himself when he and Boag visited the head office, demanding to re-examine the accident site and implying Hemingway was suppressing crucial health and safety information.'

'I'll have a word with him.'

Douglas put a hand up. 'No, don't do that. Decent detectives always have to piss somebody off.

If you and Calder hadn't ruffled any feathers last year, we'd still have an evil serial killer on the loose cosying up to half the top brass at Police Scotland.'

Dani nodded, she couldn't argue with that.

'No, what worried me was the praise that the CEO heaped on DI Boag. Apparently, he was affable, cooperative and didn't ask any questions Hemingway objected to. In other words, no fucking use whatsoever as a chief investigating officer.'

Dani's eyes darted back and forth but she said nothing.

'So what are we looking at here, Danielle? A senior detective who is in the pocket of one of the most influential businessmen in Glasgow, or one who is simply not up to the job?'

The DCI squirmed in her seat.

'Come on then, which is it to be?'

Chapter 21

'I thought Alice was investigating this angle, Ma'am?' Phil asked pleasantly, as they entered the impressive foyer of St Mungo's College of Music. 'She's a superb interviewer.'

'I've asked her to concentrate on the appointment diaries and list of ex-lovers that Kenneth Rachmann provided us with. I think it's a crucial line of inquiry.'

Dani introduced herself at the reception desk. The principal had provided them with an office on the ground floor to operate from. They would be interviewing all of Vicki's work colleagues and students in turn.

'I want you to ask the questions, Phil,' she said pointedly, as they settled behind the desk. 'I'll chip in if I feel I need to. If you sense a witness may be lying, don't hesitate to push them further. It doesn't matter if we upset people, a woman is dead.'

'What's this?' Phil asked in a jokey tone, 'back to training college?'

'Let's just get through these interviews,' Dani replied, 'and then we can have a proper talk.'

Most of the colleagues they spoke with knew Vicki Kendrick in a purely professional capacity. A handful of the women also went to the musician's house for dinner parties maybe once a month at most. They all stressed that Vicki was often away on tour, which meant maintaining regular contact with her was difficult.

Kendrick's students had obviously held her in high regard. A couple were in tears for most of the interview. She'd been an inspiration to many young Scottish musicians, it seemed.

None of Kendrick's girlfriends knew of any recent lovers. The last one they mentioned was a man called Alain Mercier who she met in Paris in 2011. Dani recognised this name from Rachmann's list. Apparently, he'd come over to Glasgow and stayed with Vicki at her flat on several occasions. But the relationship had fizzled out by the start of 2013.

Dani let Phil drive them back to Pitt Street.

'None of those relationships seemed to have been particularly serious,' Phil added. 'Even the friendships.'

'No, and we certainly aren't any closer to finding out who she would have invited over her threshold last Thursday evening. Let in through the back door, perhaps.' Dani sighed heavily and glanced out of the passenger window. 'This was a person she wanted to keep secret from the world.'

Phil cleared his throat. 'Ma'am, what did you mean when you said we'd talk properly later? Am I in some kind of trouble?'

Dani twisted round in her seat. 'DCS Douglas gave me a grilling yesterday. He wanted to know why you were so soft on Raymond Hemingway during the Tony McRae investigation. He wanted to know if you were taking bribes or are simply incompetent.'

Phil gripped the steering wheel so tightly his knuckles had gone white. 'Who grassed me up to Douglas? Was it Andy?'

'No, Hemingway is a golfing pal of the new DCC. He waxed lyrical to him about how gentle and caring you'd been. That made Douglas immediately suspicious. He's seeing corruption everywhere after the Suter case. I was forced to say I believed it was the latter, but that I would take you under my wing and give you some intensive training in the field. I said the buck stopped with me because you were my man. I think I've bought you three months of probation. But if this is going to work I'm going to need you to tell me the truth.'

'What do you mean, *tell you the truth*?'

'Andy did a check on your bank account.'

Phil bumped the car up onto a layby without indicating and slammed to a halt. '*He did what?*'

'He didn't understand why you were treading so carefully with Hemingway either. It crossed his mind you may have taken some kind of incentive. Then he saw the money in your account.'

'The £5,000.'

'Yeah.' Dani was feeling less sure of herself.

'How long have we worked together?'

'Ten years.' Dani could tell that Phil was shaking with anger. 'I just thought that with your circumstances being changed, you might be under increased pressure at home…,'

'And since I lied about my affair with Fiona, you've never really trusted me. Isn't that the truth?'

Dani blinked several times. 'Yes, that's probably right.'

'Despite swotting away for my Inspector exams and jumping through every hoop I'm given, it's still Andy who's the bloody golden boy.'

Dani said nothing, a horrible knot forming in her stomach.

'That money was from Charles Riddell. It's for Maisie's first year at Glasgow University. It covers her rent and food. It's a lot of cash, but that's what it costs these days. My Sorcha has a student loan for all that, but then her mother and I work for the public sector and can't afford to support her. We aren't all oil company hot-shots like Charles. Who, as we know from our investigation a few years back, likes to deal in cash. He deposited the money at the West Princes Street branch himself, when he was over for a conference. But if you don't believe me, just give him a call. I'm sure he'd be overjoyed to hear from you again.' Phil's tone was dripping with bitterness and cold irony.

Dani put her hand on his arm. He flinched. 'I'm sorry, Phil. I've been a complete idiot and I'm sorry.'

Chapter 22

They didn't say another word to each other on the way back to the station. Dani thought she'd give him time to cool off before broaching the issue of his re-training again.

The DCI went straight to her office and closed the door. There was a message from James on her voicemail. She wanted to listen to it in peace. His mother was feeling much better and the clients happy with his legal argument. He'd be on his way back to Glasgow in the next few days.

Dani smiled with relief. She wanted him in the flat when she got home at the end of the day. This situation with Phil was exactly the kind of scenario where you needed a partner to spill your guts out to. They'd hold you tight and tell you it wasn't your fault. Tears were beginning to form in her eyes when Alice knocked at the door.

'Come in!'

'Is this a bad time, Ma'am?' The DS eyed her boss warily.

'No, go ahead.'

'I've been working my way through that list of boyfriends Vicki's agent supplied us with.'

Dani pulled out her notes. 'A name from it cropped up in our interviews this afternoon. Alain Mercier.'

'That's interesting, because I've just come off the phone from him.'

'Take a seat.'

Alice made herself comfortable. 'Vicki had a handful of brief love affairs since her divorce but this

Alain chap seemed like the most serious of them. I called him at work. He's the floor manager at one of the opera houses in Paris. Thankfully, his English is very good. He met Vicki in 2011 when she was performing there. They went out to dinner a few times and Alain came to Glasgow and stayed in her house.'

'Did he know that Vicki was dead?'

'No and it seemed to come as a terrible shock. I'm sure it was genuine. He's staging an opera at the moment anyway and claims he's not left Paris for weeks, let alone the country.'

'We can get our French colleagues to check that out.'

'Alain says their relationship ended because of the distance between them and their work commitments. I asked if he knew if she was seeing anyone else. He said they'd not been in touch for eighteen months.'

Dani sighed deeply. 'Then this lead is also getting us nowhere.'

Alice shook her head. 'I don't know, he did suggest some intriguing things about Vicki.'

Dani raised an eyebrow.

'I pressed him on why Vicki couldn't have settled in Paris with him. From looking at her diary for the last five years it seems as if her job was fairly peripatetic. She could have lived anywhere. Alain hesitated to answer at first, but then he said it wouldn't have worked out. He wasn't happy with the level of Vicki's drinking. He'd asked her to seek help but she'd refused.'

'Maybe she did have a serious alcohol problem, or it was escalating in the last few years.'

'It wasn't just the drink Alain was unhappy about. He said that Vicki drank because of her psychological problems and that she could have gone for professional help but refused. He told her that in this day and age she could get a prescription for these kinds of issues, counselling perhaps. She didn't have to drink herself to death. Vicki simply dismissed his concerns. I sense that's why they broke up.'

Dani sat up straighter in her seat. 'What kind of problems did she have then?'

'Alain claims that Vicki had a deep, pathological fear of the dark.'

Dani screwed up her face in puzzlement. 'What, like a child?'

'Apparently, she was fine when she was busy, performing in concerts or out with friends, but when she got home to the house, Vicki's fear started to escalate, even alone with her lover she could hardly bear it. Her only solace was to drink. It smoothed away the anxieties and helped her sleep. But Alain said it was getting worse as he knew her, like a terrible dread was creeping up on her and Vicki somehow knew this threat would come at her from the dark.'

Dani put a hand up to her face. 'Oh God, that's exactly what *did* happen. Had Vicki suffered a premonition of her own death, is that why she was so desperately fearful?'

'Or she'd *always* known it was coming,' Alice commented levelly. 'When we're guilty of something awful, aren't we constantly aware that our sins will eventually catch up with us? There's really no escape.'

Dani did not reply, but she felt herself shudder.

Chapter 23

Dani had decided to clean the flat from top to bottom. She had a woman who came in twice a week, but this didn't mean that the kitchen cupboards got cleared out or the wardrobes were tidied. She wanted James to understand that she'd made an effort for him. That he'd been missed.

Her phone started to bleep. There was a message from Sam Sharpe. He and Andy were back from Ayrshire and wanted to meet to discuss developments. Dani looked at her watch, it was only half seven. She could go out for an hour and still finish her chores when she got back.

Dani changed into jeans and a blouse, pulled on her jacket and headed out of the door.

Sam was seated in a window booth at the Metro Bar in Merchant City. He had a bottled beer placed in front of him and a glass of red for her.

She slid along the bench opposite, scooping up the drink. 'Thanks. This place is a bit trendy, isn't it?'

'I'm a tourist. I just wandered in by mistake.'

Dani laughed. 'Where's Andy?'

'He went straight back home to the girls. I told him I could take it from here.'

'Oh, okay. Fine.'

'He's been away from them for a couple of nights as it is.'

'Yeah, sure, not a problem.' Dani cleared her throat. 'So, what did you find out?'

Sam filled her in on their discovery about the McNeil clan and its links to Richmond.

'Well, it's fascinating, but I still don't see the connection to Dale's murder. It could simply be a coincidence. That kind of thing happens all the time.'

'That's true, but the situation may have changed.' Sam's expression was grave.

'How do you mean?' Dani took a gulp of wine.

'I got a call from my department in Richmond today. The landlord of the house where Dale was shot returned to the city. We'd finally released the place back to him. The guy realised he'd have to do a serious clean-up job if he ever wanted to be able to get decent tenants in there again. He'd pulled out all the old fixtures and fittings. A mate of his took a mini digger out in the back yard to tidy the plot up a bit. Short-lease tenants not being known for their landscape gardening.'

'Oh hell.'

'Yep, that's right. He churned up a human body, then a second one. A man and a woman, late middle-aged. They'd not been down there long; a few weeks, maybe a month at most, according to the medical examiner at the scene. We're still waiting on the formal PM results.'

'The McNeils.' Dani finished her wine in a single swig.

'It looks that way. But we won't know until the ME can perform a proper identification.'

'So it wasn't John McNeil who killed Dale. Where does this leave your investigation?'

'Somehow I never thought it was the schoolteacher who'd done it. I reckon the McNeils were innocent bystanders who stumbled into a situation that got them killed. As for the investigation, I've not got a clue. What I do know is that house is gonna be ripped apart by my officers, piece by piece. If there's so much as a single rogue hair left in that craphole my team will find it. The landlord's not gonna have much left to rent when we've finished with it.'

'Shit,' Dani shook her head in frustration. 'It means you'll have to go back to the US straight away.'

'Of course.' Sam took a mouthful of beer, looking his companion directly in the eye. 'And I want you to come with me.'

*

Dani returned a while later with her round of drinks. 'Sorry it took so long, the trendier the bar, the worse the service.'

'It's the exact same in the States, sweetheart, don't you worry.' Sam gratefully took the bottle and emptied a quarter of it down his throat.

'Look, I appreciate the invite, but I've got the Kendrick murder to handle, and James is due home tomorrow.' Dani ran a hand through her shoulder length hair, feeling strangely awkward about the whole situation.

'I wasn't inviting you on vacation, Dani. I want your help to catch these killers. I'm certain the same person that murdered Dale also butchered his sister. The only way to crack this case is to go back to Richmond and find out who put the hit on Dale. I believe it was *me* who brought the killer to Vicki's doorstep, so the entire investigation revolves around us solving the Virginia crime.'

Dani sat back against the bench and considered this. 'We certainly aren't making much headway here. I can comfortably leave Alice and Phil in charge of the Kendrick inquiry.'

'Does that mean you think I'm right?'

'Oh, sod it. Yes, I do. I'll have to speak with my DCS but I should be able to get a flight out in the next few days.'

Sam flashed her that winning grin. 'Great. I fly back tomorrow so you'd better get packing. I'll need you on this straight away.'

Dani smiled back, wondering what the hell she'd just agreed to.

Chapter 24

It was sunny but cold. Dani had a view of the James River from her hotel room in downtown Richmond. She'd brought a file of notes on the Kendrick case with her, which was lying on the bed.

Dani winced as she recalled the conversation she'd had with James the previous morning. He'd decided to stay on in Edinburgh until she got back. Dani couldn't tell if he was pissed off or not. He'd not said much about the fact she'd be working with Sam. There wasn't much he *could* say, she supposed.

Her mobile phone started to bleep. There was a message from Sam to meet him at the department at nine. He was sending a cab to pick her up. Dani started opening and closing drawers, looking for the hairdryer, deciding to forget about her personal life for now and focus solely on the case.

*

When Bevan reached the third floor of the Virginia PD Headquarters, she found herself faced with something of a reception committee.

Sam was dressed smartly, in a dark suit and tailored shirt, open at the neck, but with high, crisp collars.

'This is DCI Dani Bevan from Police Scotland.' Sam nodded towards his colleagues, 'Dani, I'd like to introduce you to Detectives Cassie Sanchez and Gabe Kelly. Gabe was with Dale on the callout the night he was killed.'

Dani stepped forward and shook their hands. Cassie Sanchez was an attractive brunette in her late thirties, amply built but with a very pretty face.

The DCI knew this lady had been Dale's girlfriend before his death. Gabe Kelly was in his forties, tall and fair-haired.

'Since the discovery of the bodies in the back yard, the internal disciplinary inquiry into Gabe's actions on the night Dale was killed has been dropped,' Sam explained. 'I managed to persuade the board that Dale was clearly connected to something going on at that house and had a motive for ordering Gabe to wait outside. Thankfully, I've got him back on the case.'

Dani smiled at the detective. 'That's good news. It means we can concentrate on the important stuff.'

Cassie pulled across some chairs, a determined look on her face. 'Let's get started, shall we?'

'Has the Medical Examiner's report come back on the bodies yet?' Dani asked.

'Yes,' Sam replied, opening up a screen on his computer. 'We are definitely looking at one male and one female cadaver; aged over fifty. Their bodies had been in the ground for three weeks, but the pair had been dead much longer, possibly even a couple of years.'

Dani crinkled her brow. 'How come?'

'The ME reckons they were frozen. There's a large chest freezer in the basement of the house. The techs are testing it right now. It looks like it'd been locked shut for some considerable time.'

'*Jesus.* Could the ME identify the original cause of death?'

'Yeah, the flesh had all but decayed to nothing, the process having been sped up by the de-frosting process.'

Dani grimaced, feeling her stomach churn.

'But the initial wounds damaged the bone, so we can pin-point the cause of death as massive blunt object trauma to the head. Basically, someone bludgeoned them to death.'

'So there would have been blood, and lots of it,' Gabe put in.

'I suppose we can't be certain that the house was the original murder site,' Dani added.

'We may be able to do just that,' Sam clarified. 'The techs discovered blood stains in the kitchen. There had been an attempt to clean them up, with powerful detergents, but a certain amount had soaked down into the floorboards. Some of it was Dale's but certainly not all of it.'

'Can it be tested for DNA?'

'Not the older stuff, but at least we know the murders took place in that house, at around the time the McNeils were tenants there, just before their disappearance in 2014. The ME has used dental records to identify the bodies. It's definitely John and Rita. The couple never left Richmond at all.'

'But they were planning to,' Dani continued. 'They'd both left the jobs they held at local schools.'

'Maybe someone wasn't keen to let them do that,' Gabe commented.

Cassie screwed up her face. 'So why did Dale get a call to go to the house *two years* after the murders of the McNeils? Who was waiting there for him?'

'That's the big question, Cassie,' Sam replied sombrely. 'The techs have been all over that townhouse. The landlord had already ripped out a lot of the fittings. But there was still DNA everywhere. The problem is, we reckon there've been tenants in the place for decades. We haven't found a match on any of the DNA we've run through the system, except for Dale and the landlord, who volunteered a sample for elimination purposes.'

'So the two year old murders took place in the kitchen, then someone took the bodies down into the basement and put them in the chest freezer. Only to bring them out three weeks ago and bury them in the back garden,' Dani summarized. 'That's a week or so before someone lured Dale to the house and shot him. There was no attempt to hide Dale's body. He was left at the kitchen table to be found. Do we think we're looking at the same perp in both cases?'

Cassie's cheeks flushed up. 'How could it not be the same perp? When *three* dead bodies turn up in the exact same crime scene?'

'But two years apart and with different M.O.s,' Dani persisted. 'I'm not saying the crimes aren't connected, I'm just suggesting we keep an open mind as to whether we're looking at more than one perp, that's all.'

Sam rubbed at his freshly shaved chin, which still bore some tell-tale nicks from the razor. 'Dani's right. We haven't explained the two year gap yet. The first place we need to start is with Dale. His phone records, computer hard drive and apartment need to be taken apart.' Sam turned to Cassie. 'I won't ask you to do that, Detective Sanchez, but I want you to tell Gabe everything you can recall about Dale in the weeks leading up to his death – who he spoke to, what his mood was like, absolutely anything that springs to mind, however trivial.'

Cassie nodded her head, trying to keep her emotions in check. 'Sure, Chief. I'm onto it.'

Chapter 25

Sam and Dani headed straight to Dale's apartment. The neighbourhood wasn't the most upmarket, with a handful of grocery stores operating on a long sidewalk in which most of the buildings were shut up.

Dale's place was above one of the stores that were still in business. Sam slipped the key into the lock and pushed the door open against the force of a pyramid of junk mail balanced on the mat behind. The apartment was small but functional and reasonably pleasant.

'Dale was also supporting his family out in Midlothian. This must have been all he could afford,' Sam explained.

'It's not a great advert for divorce,' Dani added dryly. 'Your place is far nicer.'

'Yeah, well, Janie always worked. She used her own money to re-settle out in Vancouver. I pay alimony for the boys, of course, but my ex-wife always supported herself. Now she's remarried I'm off the hook anyways.'

'Sorry, I wasn't intending to pry.'

'Not a problem, Dani. We know each other well enough to share that kind of thing. It's not something I'd discuss with just anybody.'

Dani ventured into the bedroom. The bed was made and clothing piled up on shelves in the fitted wardrobe. Sam came in behind her and started opening the drawers in the bedside cabinet. They worked in silence for a while.

'What's the family house like in Midlothian?' Dani

suddenly asked.

'Real nice. Not a mansion or anything, but a comfortable family home. Like I said, the Faulkners had plenty of barbecues in their yard for colleagues at the department. The kids were safe enough to play in that neighbourhood when they were younger.'

Dani sat back on her haunches. 'Dale would have struggled to have even one of his kids stay the night here. How long ago was the divorce?'

'Dale moved out maybe just under two years ago, then the divorce came through a year later. He's been seeing Cassie about six months.'

'So Faulkner didn't leave his wife for Cassie?'

Sam shook his head. 'Definitely not. I don't even think the two detectives knew each other back then.'

'Then why did Dale leave his wife, for this? Did Toni kick him out, was she seeing someone?'

'I had a long chat to Dale about it. The separation was his idea, or so he claimed.' Sam ran a hand through his thick sandy hair. 'But I believed him, because Toni was really cut up about it. They'd been having problems for a while but she called me several times during that period in tears, asking what was going on in Dale's head.'

'Did you know what was going on in his head?'

'I thought I did, 'cause I'd been through the same thing. But thinking about it now, Dale's situation wasn't the same. Janie was always pissed at me about the time I spent at work. She didn't want that life any longer and I suppose I didn't love her enough to give it up. But Toni didn't give Dale an ultimatum like that. She wanted him back, cop or not.'

Dani glanced about her at the tiny, barred window and the damp patches on the walls. 'Then why the hell did he leave her to come and live in this dump?'

Sam blinked several times. 'I don't know.'

'The separation happened two years ago?'

'At the same time the McNeils were killed.' Sam's voice was serious. 'Do you think there's a connection?'

'I don't know yet, but maybe Dale was involved in something that goes back several years.'

'Yeah, I think we need to accept that. Cassie isn't going to like it.'

'I'm amazed you let her work the case. She's hardly impartial.'

Sam shrugged his shoulders. 'Cassie's an excellent cop and she knew Dale better than any of us did these last few months. Besides, she wants to feel involved.'

Dani nodded and said nothing. She understood having a strong sense of loyalty to your team. It was up to her to make sure it didn't prejudice the inquiry.

The DCI continued searching through the wardrobe. There were shoeboxes in there with photographs of Toni and their three children at the house in Midlothian, when they were very little. One of the boxes was older than the others. It was battered and bore the logo for Dunlop green flash trainers.

Dani glanced over at Sam. 'Did you have Dunlop trainers over here when you were a kid?'

Sam looked puzzled. 'Huh?'

That was all she needed to know. 'I may have found something.'

Dani lifted the box onto the bed and carefully removed the lid. Inside, there was a pile of old photos, letters and postcards. She took out a few and handed them to her colleague, Dani examined the rest herself.

There were photographs of the entire Faulkner clan; Magnus, Sue, Vicki and Dale. In some of them,

Sue's mother, Maeve, featured. The grandmother was standing beside them with her huge beehive of orangey-red hair. A few shots were of the family at the beach on a sunny day. Dani flipped the pictures over. 'Saltcoats, July '71', was scrawled on the back.

'I've got some postcards here,' Sam said quietly. 'They're from Maeve Lomas to her daughter. It seems like she kept the family updated on how Vicki was getting on at school, although the comments are very brief. The cards started being sent to their new home in Midlothian in 1977. The last one was received in '82.'

'So the family *were* still in touch during those years?'

'Even if it was only Maeve and her daughter.'

'I bet Vicki didn't know her grandmother was sending them. Maybe she and Sue had a private agreement.'

'But Dale got hold of them in the end,' Sam muttered. 'Perhaps he found the correspondence when his folks died ten years back.'

Dani handed Sam the photographs, their fingers momentarily touching as she did so. 'There's one shot here of a family lunch. There are a couple of men at the table along with the Faulkners. I assume they must be Magnus's brothers.'

Sam turned it over and read out the date. "December, 1974".

'Just a few months before the Faulkners left Crosbie Farm for good.' She gazed at their cheerful faces closely. 'Do those people look like they're in debt? As if the family is about to be broken up forever, and they'll have to leave the land they've farmed for generations, never coming back as long as they live?' Dani could feel tears prickling her eyes.

Sam took the pictures out of her hand and placed them back in the box, which he set aside on the cabinet. He put a hand up to her soft cheek and swept back a strand of stray hair. His lips covered hers, kissing her tenderly at first and then more deeply, as he levered her backwards onto the bed.

He placed his palm on her smooth stomach, sliding it up under her blouse to gently cup her breast. 'I've missed you,' he whispered urgently, 'I've missed you so much.'

Dani could sense the tears were now seriously close to escaping onto her cheeks. She took his hand gently and guided it away from her breast, pulling him into an embrace instead. 'I can't Sam, no matter how much I want to. I've made a promise to someone, a commitment.'

The American pulled away, his face flushed pink. '*We* made promises to each other once,' he snapped. 'You didn't worry too much about breaking those.'

Dani took a deep breath. 'I know. That's why it's important that I keep them now. I don't want to hurt anybody else.'

Sam shifted so that he was sitting on the edge of the bed, his back to her. 'It isn't a question of who happens to be in line when you decide to start playing house, Dani. It's about the person that makes your heart pound like a jack hammer when you set eyes on them. The one you know you're meant to be with.' He turned back around and put a finger underneath her chin, tipping up her face so her eyes met his. 'If you were married to this guy, I'd back right off. But you aren't, so in my book, nothing's decided yet. I love you, Dani. If you decide you love me back then I'll marry you in a heartbeat. We can set up home wherever you wish - Scotland or the States. I can take my pension anytime, so it's up to you. Just say the word.'

Chapter 26

Dani rummaged around in the mini bar. She found a tiny bottle of red wine and wrenched it open, pouring the liquid out into a plastic cup and taking a swig.

'*Damn it*,' she muttered under her breath, kicking off her shoes and lying back against the fluffy pillows. This was just what she didn't need right now. A shitload of complications.

At this precise moment, she was furious with Sam. Dani had left Dale's apartment, hailed a cab and returned straight to her hotel, telling the detective she'd see him again in the morning.

Her phone lay on the duvet next to her right leg, buzzing insistently at regular intervals but remaining untouched. '*Shit*,' she fumed again, picking it up and glancing at the notifications. Most of them were texts from James, but one was a missed call from Andy.

Dani hit the speed dial.

'Evening, Ma'am. How was the journey?'

'Aye, fine. Any update on developments?' she grumbled.

'Nothing significant, yet. Phil noticed a CCTV camera was installed to keep watch on the communal gardens behind Park Crescent. We've been onto the management agency to get the disc from the day Kendrick was murdered released ASAP.'

Dani sat up straighter. 'Great, that's real progress. Make sure the DCS knows that Phil uncovered the lead. If that camera recorded our man going into the back of Vicki's place, we might actually be able to get somewhere.'

'How are you and Sam coping with the responsibility of flying the flag for transatlantic relations?'

'Don't even joke about it. Yeah, we're making a start. There's plenty of forensic material at the crime scene and the bodies have been officially identified as those of John and Rita McNeil.'

'That sounds like headway. Just don't do anything I wouldn't.'

'What's that supposed to mean?'

Andy laughed. 'Nothin' at all! Give my regards to Sam, okay?'

'Yeah, I will, and thanks for keeping me posted.'

'Not a problem, goodnight.'

Dani felt better after their conversation, more settled. She flicked onto her messages and sent a text to James, telling him that she'd got there safely and she loved him. Then she glanced at the contents of the plastic cup, decided the wine was disgusting and got up to pour the remainder down the sink of the ensuite bathroom. Dani rinsed the cup out and replaced the contents with water, determined to get a decent night's sleep and put all her emotional energy from now on into solving these three murders.

*

Cassie and Gabe were with Sam when Dani arrived at the department the following morning. It was a relief for the DCI not to be alone with him just yet.

Sam had the contents of the shoe box spread out on his desk. Cassie Sanchez was examining each item carefully.

'So Dale never showed you these photos or cards? He didn't mention the childhood he spent in

Scotland?'

The woman shook her head of dark, sleek hair. 'He never said much about his past, which I thought was because he didn't want to keep mentioning Toni and the kids. As far as I knew, Dale was born and bred in Richmond.'

'I called Toni last night,' Sam straightene up and addressed the group. 'She had no idea that Dale had this stuff stashed away either.' He cleared his throat awkwardly. 'I asked her about the split. She gave me some dates of when Dale started to talk in terms of a separation. Toni believes it came from out of left field around the summer of 2014. She was devastated.'

'Isn't that around the time the McNeils went missing? Maybe that's when Dale's past began catching up with him,' Dani suggested. 'He may have wanted to keep his family out of it.'

'By totally pushing them away?' Gabe looked unconvinced. 'Sorry, Cas, but Dale was always a real family man. He sure loved his wife and kids when I first met him.'

'Then he'd want to protect them, at all costs, wouldn't he?' Sam continued the line of thought.

Cassie took a deep breath. 'But Dale was happy and settled when he and I got together. We'd talked about marriage. I don't see what this terrible danger could have been.'

'When did you and Dale hook up?' Sam asked.

'It was the end of last August, when we went on a department training camp together.'

'Perhaps Dale thought the situation had settled down by then,' Dani added. 'He believed it was safe to start a new relationship, to begin living again.'

'Then he received the emergency callout, with the address given as that of the McNeils,' Sam muttered.

'No wonder he wanted me to stay in the car while

he went inside to check things out. Maybe he thought the McNeils still lived there,' Gabe commented.

'Dale certainly knew them both,' Dani said levelly. 'Then that's where we need to start.'

Chapter 27

'What happened to the McNeils' stuff?' Gabe perched on the edge of his boss's desk. 'They went missing in the fall of 2014. They'd quit their jobs and their lease was up. Someone killed them and stashed the bodies in the freezer in the basement, then padlocked it up tight. But what happened to their gear? They'd been the longest tenants resident in that place. After they disappeared, the landlord couldn't get anyone to rent the joint for more than a few weeks at a time. Both houses next door have stood empty for months. So where are all their belongings? There should be photographs, books, clothes – furniture even?'

'Could the killer have got rid of it all?' Cassie suggested.

'It would have been one hell of a job,' Sam surmised. 'Even in that scuzzy neighbourhood someone would surely have noticed. I can't see the perp taking that kind of risk.'

'Maybe there wasn't much left to dispose of.' Dani glanced at each of the American detectives in turn. 'The McNeils were planning to leave Richmond. That much we know for certain. What if they'd already packed up and sent the majority of their stuff on to wherever they were headed. They may have had some hand luggage still to take on the journey but that wouldn't have been too difficult for the killer to get rid of.'

Sam rose to his feet. 'What are the main shipping companies that operate out of the city?'

'There's a big USA Freight building out near Highland Springs,' Gabe said.

'And there's a UPS office in the centre of town,' Cassie added. 'My folks used it to send my gear on when I went up to College.'

Sam rubbed his chin. 'Yeah, Janie used UPS to get Nathan's stuff down to the Virginia State campus last year.'

'Then we need to check them all,' Dani said decisively. 'We'll have to view their dispatch records for the first half of 2014. Just in case the McNeils had got ahead of themselves and sent on their belongings in advance. Some of these companies even store the luggage too, don't they?'

'Yes,' said Sam, already looking up the contact details on his computer. 'They sure do.'

*

Detective Sharpe had left Cassie and Gabe in charge of calling round the shipping agents of Richmond. He and Dani were heading out to the school where John McNeil had taught Geography for the best part of a decade.

Dani's father had been a primary school headmaster on the Scottish island where she grew up, but she knew next to nothing about the American education system. The downtown Richmond High School they were visiting was buzzing with activity. The halls were full of students who looked much older than their British counterparts. Dani thought this was because they weren't in uniforms, but instead wore a colourful mix-match of jeans, sports sweaters and Nike sneakers.

The principal was youngish. Dani decided maybe early forties at most. She let Sam take the lead with the questions.

'Mr Wilson -,' Sharpe began.

'Call me Mike.'

'Okay, *Mike*. We're investigating a double homicide involving an ex-employee at your school.'

The principal sat up dead straight. '*Holy smoke.*'

'Mr John McNeil and his wife, Rita, were discovered buried in the back yard of the house they rented on the Southside. Their bodies had been frozen directly after death, sometime in 2014, and then interred within the last few weeks.'

The man had gone deathly pale. 'I knew we hadn't heard from John after he left, but I had absolutely no idea...,'

'Our forensic tests suggest that the McNeils were killed not long after quitting their respective jobs. Did you know where the couple were planning to go next? Did John have another teaching job lined up?'

Wilson shook his head slowly. 'No, I got the distinct impression they were both retiring. I believe John told me they were planning on doing some travelling before making any hard and fast decisions about where to settle down. I certainly wasn't called on to write a reference for him. The couple had no children, no extended family to speak of. They were free to do as they wished. That's why I wasn't really surprised when I'd heard nothing more. I assumed they were seeing the world. It made me quite envious, as it happens.' He gulped, looking suddenly nauseous.

'Have you got John's employee records on file?'

'Of course, it was only two years ago. I'll ask one of the secretaries to print them off for you. Will there be a funeral? I'd like to go. I know some of John's ex-students would also wish to attend. He was much loved as a teacher. His subject knowledge was excellent and he clearly enjoyed sharing his enjoyment of the topic with others, you know?'

'Yeah, I do know, Mike. I'll get someone to inform you when the funeral can take place. You just might be the guy organising it. We couldn't trace any other family or friends who showed an interest in paying their respects.'

The principal regained his composure. 'Then leave that with us. The High School will give John and Rita a decent send-off. God knows, it's the very least we can do.'

Chapter 28

'It restores your faith in human nature.' Sam glanced across at his passenger as they drove towards the suburb of Midlothian.

Dani grunted an acknowledgment, apparently engrossed in the files that the school secretary had given them.

'I mean, the guy didn't have to agree to organise a funeral.'

Dani looked up. 'But if Dale Faulkner had no family or friends, you'd have done it for him, even though he was simply your employee, wouldn't you?'

Sam considered this. 'Yeah, but Dale was also my friend, so it's hard to say for sure.'

'If he was a member of your team you would have done. I know you would.'

'Yeah, maybe so. You feel responsible, I suppose.'

Dani turned and gazed out of the window, as one tree-lined block blended into another. 'After we split up, there was this case back in Glasgow. It involved the disappearance of Andy's uncle a few years ago.'

'I know, I read about it.'

Dani flicked her head back, eyeing him carefully.

'I told you before. I was following your cases in the press.' He remained facing dead ahead.

'Then you'll be aware that a young policewoman was killed in the process of the investigation. It was me who requested she join the team. The girl just wasn't ready and I didn't see it.'

Sam nodded slowly. 'It was the closest I've come to getting in touch again, when I read about that. I knew you'd be cut up. I wanted to tell you it wasn't your fault. It was that *shithead* who mowed her down.' He gripped the steering wheel tightly.

'Why didn't you?'

'I was worried you'd moved on, wouldn't take my call. That woulda hurt real bad.'

'But you sought me out this time?'

'There was this case to give me a reason. Besides, Joy and Bill wouldn't stop nagging me until I'd picked up the phone and dialled the numbers.'

Dani chuckled. 'I can imagine.' She leaned her head against his shoulder. 'But I'm glad you did. However this situation turns out, I'm really glad you did.'

Sam spotted the house and pulled up at the kerb. 'This is where Toni Faulkner lives and where she and Dale brought up the kids.'

'Nice place.'

They both got out of the car and approached the front door.

Toni answered after only a couple of seconds. She smiled warmly when she saw Sam, but cast Dani a more suspicious look.

'This is DCI Dani Bevan from Glasgow. She's the one who's investigating the murder of Dale's sister.'

'You'd better come in.' Tony led them into the spacious sitting room. 'I can't get used to the idea of Dale even having a sister. That woman was my children's aunt – a close blood relative. It's tough to get your head around.'

'It must be,' Dani added.

Toni turned to Sam. 'Did you get a chance to speak with her before she died? What was Vicki like?'

'She was clever, talented and very dignified. I'm sure the kids would have liked her. She would've been a great role model.'

Toni sighed. 'We've already watched a few of her performances on YouTube. I can't believe that beautiful music was produced by a sister of D le's. He was practically tone deaf. You know what he was like trying to sing Christmas carols!' She chu kled good-naturedly. 'But I could see the resembla ce – something about the eyes, I thought.'

'Yeah, I could see that too,' Sam replied softly

Dani was beginning to feel like a gooseberry She subtly cleared her throat. 'Toni, I know that Dale never revealed anything about his life in Scot and, but can you tell us what his parents were like Did you know Magnus and Sue well before they died '

The woman turned towards Dani, al most begrudgingly. 'Of course I did. They were the ids' grandparents. Dale's folks were quiet. They did t go out much, not like mine, who are members of very retirement club going. If Magnus and Sue had still been alive, I don't think Dale would have left s. I know that sounds weird, but he adored them a d it would have broken their hearts to see our f mily split up.'

'But they'd allowed their own family to get lit,' Sam put in. 'Magnus and Sue left Vicki behind.'

Toni frowned. 'I still can't really accept hat. You've never met a more family oriented couple han them. Magnus and Sue were old-fashioned. Di orce was a dirty word to them. My brother and I are oth separated now and my folks just get on wi it. That's modern life, they say. But it would ave broken Dale's parents, I know it would.'

'Sometimes people over-compensate,' Dani offered. 'If they've experienced a broken ome themselves, they do everything in their power to eep their family together in the future.'

Toni nodded. 'Yeah, you could be right. Bec use there's no doubt they left their little girl behi d. I could see so much of the Faulkners in her.' She tutted. 'Imagine how Vicki would have felt, kno ving about all the time and care Magnus and Sue took over our kids as they were growing up – they loved them just as much as we did. She'd have been heartbroken they never did the same for her.'

Dani shuffled forward. 'Perhaps *that's* why Vicki never came to visit when she was in the States. We all have ways of protecting ourselves emotionally. It may have been far too painful to see Magnus, Sue and Dale getting on with their lives without her.'

'Well, I can't claim to know how Vicki felt,' Toni continued. 'But *I* certainly couldn't have handled it.'

'No,' Dani said with feeling, 'neither could I.'

Chapter 29

When they returned to the police department, Cassie and Gabe were still busy making phone calls.

Dani sat down opposite Sam at his desk. 'I don't think Toni Faulkner liked me very much.'

'She warmed to you towards the end. Toni's okay, she's just been through a lot these last few months. It's hard for her to trust people she's not met before.'

'It was interesting what she had to say about Magnus and Sue. Up until this point, their personalities have been a mystery. I can imagine them now as doting grandparents, living a comfortable but quiet life here in Richmond. What I can't imagine, is the Magnus and Sue who lived at Crosbie Farm, up to their eyes in debt, fleeing their creditors and leaving a young child behind in the process.'

'Folks change. The couple Toni knew were decades on from that situation in Scotland. They'd reinvented themselves.'

Dani quietly considered this, only glancing up when Cassie strode towards her boss, the flicker of a smile on her face.

'I've got something.' She dropped down into a seat, placing her notebook on the desk. 'We tried all the big operations in the city. None had a record of the McNeils sending any shipments. So we started trying companies further afield. I've just come off the line from a firm in Norfolk who specialise in trans-Atlantic haulage. They say they'd run an advertising campaign in the Richmond area during 2013, that's how the McNeils must have found out about them.'

Sam shuffled forward. 'What have you got?'

'Norfolk-Atlantic had a record of sending a container full of crates belonging to a J.A McNeil of Richmond, VA in June 2014. It cost the client two thousand dollars and included six months storage at the other end.'

'Where was the container sent to?' Dani could feel her heart in her mouth.

Cassie glanced back at her notes. 'It travelled via Liverpool, arriving at the port of Greenock on the 2nd July 2014.'

Dani whistled. '*Bloody hell.* The McNeils were going to Scotland.'

*

'I suppose it makes sense,' Sam said levelly. 'John McNeil was always fascinated by his family's roots in Scotland.'

'Perhaps they were planning to travel around for six months before settling somewhere in the homeland.' Dani had Cassie's notebook in front of her and already had her mobile phone poised to dial. 'That six month contract would have been up at the start of 2015, let's hope to God we aren't too late.'

'We still need to try.'

Dani nodded and hit the speed dial.

'Morning, Ma'am, what's up?'

'We've had a major development, Andy. The McNeils were planning to spend their retirement in Scotland before they were killed. They sent a shipment of their belongings on ahead of them, which they placed in storage. The company the crates were delivered to is called Caledonian Removals Ltd. They're on the Rutherglen Industrial Estate. I need you and Phil to go out there right now and check if they've still got the stuff. If they haven't, find out what's happened to it.'

'Understood, Ma'am. I'll get back to you later

Dani ended the call, turning to the American detectives gathered around her. 'I just hope the McNeils' stuff hasn't ended up in the sodding incinerator.'

Sam placed a hand on her shoulder. 'All we can do now is to wait for Andy to get in touch. But I've got a lot of faith in the guy to locate it.'

*

Phil was driving. The rush hour traffic was heavy. It took nearly an hour to reach the industrial complex in Rutherglen. Caledonian Removals was hard to miss. The company took up several hangars, each painted a deep, royal blue.

Andy had called ahead to ask the manager to keep the office open for them. Phil pushed through the glazed double doors and displayed his warrant card.

'DI Boag and DS Calder. We're here about the McNeil shipment from the USA.'

The manager stood up and offered his hand. 'Aye, I've brought out the paperwork for you.' He shook his bald, shiny head. 'I'm afraid the storage contract expired on the 3rd January 2015.'

Andy took a step forward, finding it hard to hide his frustration. 'What exactly does that mean, sir? Where are the boxes now?'

'Hold your horses, Detective Sergeant, that's what I'm trying to pin down.' He swivelled round a computer screen. 'The items were booked in on the system on the 3rd July '14, see?'

Phil nodded dutifully, sensing they'd need to jump through some hoops before getting their answer.

'Once the six months had expired, the system

generated an automatic e-mail reminder to the client, either to extend the storage period or come and collect the goods.'

'The clients were dead by that time, their frozen bodies stuffed in a freezer.' Andy looked daggers at the man crouched before them.

'Well, in the event of the reminder being pinged back to the server, a letter would then be generated.'

Andy rolled his eyes. 'How the hell long does that process go on for?'

The manager turned back to the screen. 'The last reminder was sent out in October. Then the client was marked unresponsive – see?'

'Okay, so that was about five months ago, what happened then?' Even Phil was struggling to keep his cool.

'You'd be surprised how long it takes some of our customers to come and collect their property. If a house sale is dragging on, it can take months or even years. Whether we hold on to the stuff really depends on the capacity in our warehouses. Since 2014, business has picked up – what with the housing market getting a small bounce. But it's still not enough to get us back to pre-2008 levels. That's when we invested in the additional warehouse.'

It was taking all of Andy's willpower not to grab the man by his grubby collar and shake him senseless. *'Where's the McNeils' stuff?'* He hissed instead.

'I'll have to get the warehouse manager to confirm, but judging by these dates, I would say the McNeils' consignment will have been moved to the holding hangar, where it will await pulping. Whether it has already been pulped, remains to be seen.'

'Just get the keys for the hangar, sir,' Andy said through gritted teeth. 'We'll check if the boxes are still there.'

'Oh, well, I suppose we could do that,' the manager responded laconically, reaching in ɔ a drawer for a master set of keys.

'If that guy doesn't get a move on, the only ɪing getting pulped will be him,' Andy muttered to Ph ɪ, as they followed the man out of the door.

Chapter 30

It was late afternoon in Richmond, Virginia. Dani had returned to the hotel to pack her bags. She'd received the call from Andy a couple of hours earlier. The McNeils' luggage had been removed from its allocated storage area and dumped into a kind of store room, where eventually it would have been taken away and destroyed. The consignment had got split up. It took Andy and Phil quite some time to locate the right boxes. But they were pretty sure now they had them all.

There was a knock at the door. Dani smoothed down her hair at the vanity table mirror and opened it.

'Are you all set?' Sam asked.

'Yes, but come in for a minute.' Dani went to stand by the window, where there was still some evening light streaked over the cityscape.

'Has Andy got the consignment back to your department?'

'Yes, they seized the boxes straight away and radioed for a van to come and collect the gear. I don't think Andy was prepared to let them out of his sight by that point. But they'll wait for me to arrive before opening up.'

'Sure, you'll know best what you're looking for.'

'I really think I can be of more use back in Glasgow now. I'll keep you updated on all future developments.'

'Yeah, of course you need to go back. I want to keep digging into Dale's role in all this. I can't leave my team again.'

Dani turned to face him. 'I haven't forgotten what

you said at Dale's flat.'

'But you're going home to James.'

Dani shrugged. 'You'll have to give me more time.'

Sam sighed. 'As soon as you return to him, that'll be it. I know how these things work. You're thousands of miles away from me and he's there, on the spot providing safety and security. It's human nature to settle back into the life you've already made. Nobody wants to rock the boat.'

'People choose security for good reasons, Sam.'

He took a step forward and folded Dani into his arms. 'Does anything else feel as secure as this?'

She held him tightly. 'No, it doesn't.'

'What I said holds true. Just don't leave me hanging forever.'

Dani raised her face from his chest. 'Wouldn't you be happier here in Richmond, with the people you know? I got the impression that Toni might want your friendship to develop into something more. She's a good lady who could care for you and your boys.'

Sam's eyes locked with hers. 'I don't love Toni Faulkner, I love you. Why do you keep wanting to complicate things? Try to analyse your feelings properly over the next few weeks and choose the right person for *you*. I sure as hell don't want to push you into something that isn't what you truly want.'

Dani pulled him close, just wishing she knew what on earth that was.

*

Dani met her team in the evidence room located in the basement of the Pitt Street Headquarters.

Alice Mann smiled at her as she entered. 'Welcome back, Ma'am.'

'Thanks Alice, what have we got here?'

Phil took the lead. 'There are seven crates in total, each one full to the brim. We'll need at least one officer on each.'

Dani surveyed the scene. 'Where's Andy?'

'He's checking out the CCTV footage from the back of Park Crescent. We got the disc from the management agency this afternoon.'

'Good, he'll need to stay on that. Right then, let's get started folks. We're looking for personal papers, notebooks, photographs, letters - anything like that. Bag it up as soon as you find it.'

'What about clothing, ornaments, that kind of stuff?' Dan Clifton looked utterly daunted by the task.

'Go through the pockets of any jackets or trousers you lay your hands on. Other than that, try to make a judgement. We're looking for anything that might tie the McNeils to the Faulkner family.'

'You heard the DCI,' Phil piped up. 'So get stuck in.'

Chapter 31

It was nearly midnight when Dani got back to her flat. The hallway was cold and empty. James obviously hadn't returned yet and the place was beginning to feel the way it did before the lawyer had ever moved in.

Dani was too exhausted to dwell on the thought. She discarded her shoes, dumped the case in the sitting room and stumbled straight into bed.

She woke to the sound of insistent knocking. Still in yesterday's clothes, Dani threw some water on her face and jogged down the hallway to open up.

'Sorry, Ma'am, I knew you'd be jet-lagged but thought you'd want me to show you this straight away.' Andy waggled an A4 sized envelope at her.

'Come in, I'll prepare some coffee.'

Andy made himself comfortable at the kitchen table. 'Phil is down in the evidence room with Dan and the rest of the DCs. They've been at it since first thing.'

Dani yawned. 'Great, I'll be there myself in an hour or so.' She placed a cafétiere and a couple of mugs between them. 'So, what have you got?'

Andy slid a glossy photograph out of the envelope. 'It's a screen shot from the CCTV footage.' He handed it to her. 'It's not the clearest image you've ever seen, but I'm willing to bet that's our guy.'

Dani was looking at a picture of the gardens of Park Crescent, with the bushes and path that ran along the rear of the houses visible at the edge of the shot. A figure, of average height and build, with a hooded jacket pulled up to obscure their head and face was entering the back gate of what the DCI assumed was Vicki Kendrick's property. 'It doesn't provide us with very much.'

'No.' Andy tapped the person shown in the shot. 'But it gives us our murderer and the time they entered the Kendrick property.'

Dani glanced at the time recorded by the CCTV. It was frozen at 7.04pm on the evening Vicki was killed. 'Say this person was invited to drinks at 7pm. Vicki lets him in through the back door and they share the best part of a bottle of wine. I reckon that puts our time of death at past eight o'clock – maybe eight thirty?'

Andy sipped his coffee. 'Aye, I'd agree with that. It fits with the timescale we've got from the PM.'

Dani examined the grainy image again. 'I just don't think it's possible to get any kind of ID from this picture.' She sighed.

Andy placed his cup down and eyed his boss carefully. 'Did you have a word with Phil about the money in his account?'

Dani slapped a hand to her forehead. 'Yes, I did. Sorry, Andy, I didn't get a chance to tell you about it before I flew off to the States. There's nothing to worry about. The money was deposited by Charles Riddell. It's for Maisie's first year at university. She's come back to Glasgow to study and will be spending part of her time with Fiona and Phil.'

'I reckoned you must have had a word, because Phil's been incredibly cooperative and efficient these last few days. It's as if our tiff over Hemingway Shipyards never happened.'

'Well, I told him he needed to pull his socks up in the field. The DCS thinks he's gone soft after years spent on deskwork. I'm glad he took my pep talk to heart. I thought I'd lost his respect forever.'

Andy tipped his head to one side. 'So you

checked with Riddell?'

Dani crinkled her brow. 'No, not exactly. I took Phil's word for it. Then we had developments in the case that took my attention away from the situation.'

Andy shrugged his shoulders. 'I just wonder why Charles would put the money in Phil's account. Riddell must be used to paying maintenance for Maisie. He's been split from Fiona for many years. So why didn't Charles put that money in his ex-wife's account? Why Phil's?'

Dani felt her stomach tighten. 'There could be any number of reasons, I suppose. But the fact is I *believed* Phil when he told me. He was so angry that I'd doubted him – he was genuinely hurt.'

Andy smiled sadly. 'He's our friend. We've known him a long time. But in this instance, we need to think like detectives and forget our history with the guy. All you need to do to be sure is give Charles Riddell a call. It's what we'd do if it was anybody else under suspicion.'

Dani closed her eyes and held the mug up to her lips. 'Yeah, you're right,' she said, with no enthusiasm whatsoever.

Chapter 32

The evidence room was a hive of activity. Most of the McNeils' property had been bagged and labelled. Much of it was household furniture and kitchen appliances, but they now had a table full of papers and documents. Dani was intent on spending the morning going through them all.

The DCI allowed Phil to debrief her on their findings so far, and how the material had been separated out. Then they heard the lift creak to a standstill at the bottom of the shaft.

DCS Douglas and a smartly dressed officer they'd never seen before stepped out. Douglas approached them at the table. 'I see you're making good progress here,' he said hollowly. He turned towards Phil. 'DI Boag, I need you to accompany me upstairs to answer a few questions.'

Phil whipped his head in Dani's direction. His eyes were filled with hurt and confusion.

Dani's throat had constricted so much she found that no words would come out.

Douglas said no more, but led the way back to the lift, with Phil trailing behind like a chastened schoolboy.

'What was that all about?' Dan asked in a stage whisper, when the men had gone.

Dani shrugged her shoulders. 'It was just routine, I expect.'

Clifton moved back to the crate he was unpacking. Dani pulled on her latex gloves, ripping open the first evidence bag and beginning to read the contents, made blurry by the tears rapidly forming in her eyes.

*

Dani carried an evidence bag back upstairs with her to the serious crime floor. When she got there, Andy was helping a shell-shocked Phil to clear out his desk.

'Can you carry on with that alone, Andy?' Dani asked. 'I'd like to have a talk with Phil in my office.'

'Sure, Ma'am. I'll take him home after, too.'

Phil walked through the door like he was in a trance. Dani guided him to the sofa. She took the soft chair opposite. 'What did Douglas say?'

'He told me that an internal investigation was being launched into my conduct. Recent new powers granted by the Chief Constable following the Souter case meant that they could examine my bank details. He said this had 'thrown up some anomalies.' Phil rested his head in both hands.

'I called Charles Riddell in Stavanger.'

Phil slowly raised his head.

'You were right. He wasn't very pleased to hear from me.'

'I expect not. You're the person who told him his daughter was dead.'

'He didn't know what I was talking about when I mentioned the money he supposedly deposited into your account for Maisie's upkeep at university. Riddell said he has a long-standing arrangement with Fiona. He's increased the standing order but that's it.'

Phil's shoulders began to shake. 'I don't know why I did it. When Nancy McRae started kicking up a stink in the press about her husband's death, I got a phone call at home. It was from a man calling himself Raymond Hemingway's public relations representative. He spun me some line about wanting good relations with the police force. He said they knew I understood how important it was to consider the bigger picture – preserving the last shipyard in Glasgow for the majority of its workers. They knew this because of my connection to Jane and her work in improving the education system across the city. He said if I was willing to be a 'friendly contact' for Hemingways, then I would receive a generous gift and they would donate 'a considerable sum' to an education charity of my choice. He never spoke about specific amounts.'

'And you agreed to this?'

'Not in so many words. A few days later, £5,000 appeared in my bank account. To be perfectly honest, I tried to ignore it. I still haven't touched it.'

'Then I sent you to interview Hemingway?'

'I wasn't being deliberately soft, or I didn't consciously make a decision to be. I genuinely thought the case against the yard wasn't strong enough to pursue.'

Dani sighed heavily. 'You'll have to tell Douglas all of this.'

'I already have. I've surrendered the money to the internal review board and agreed to make a sworn statement about the phone call I received.'

'What's going to happen to you?'

'I'm off the force, Dani. I'll receive a quarter pension but no criminal charges will be brought.'

'*Why* didn't you tell me as soon as Hemingways approached you with the bribe? I don't understand, Phil!'

'I don't understand myself. I partly agreed with the guy. It's ridiculous to jeopardise a company that brings profit and employment to Glasgow because of one man who takes a stupid risk out of hours. The money was never really the issue. Although, it would certainly have helped us. I hate having to rely on handouts from Charles Riddell. I liked the feeling of being free, if only for a little while.'

'Oh, Phil.' Dani leant forward and placed her arms around him.

To her great relief he hugged her back. 'I'll find something else, start afresh. My IT skills are still pretty hot.'

Dani nodded. 'I know, but I'm going to bloody well miss you. So will Andy.' She pushed him away so she could look him in the face. 'Will you let Calder take you home?'

'Of course. I was so angry with you both because I knew I'd let you down. Andy's got such strong principles, but he isn't always right, you know. When I've gone, I'd like you to remember that. Don't let him railroad you.'

'I won't, I promise.'

Phil gave her one last squeeze, not convinced his boss really meant that at all.

Chapter 33

With Phil gone, Dani did her best to remain focused on the papers in front of her. But it was tough. She kept glancing out of the glass partition at his empty workstation. The sight brought a huge lump to her throat and made her eyes sting.

She tried to remember what her friend, the psychologist Rhodri Morgan, always said; that people did what they did for a reason, however inexplicable their actions seemed to be. Phil clearly wanted a new start. He'd had enough of the police force, yet his conservative nature made it hard for him to make that decision unaided. Somehow, his subconscious had done the work for him, letting events take their course. At no point had he done anything to encourage Hemingways to give him the bribe, nor had he actively tried to prevent the money coming his way either.

Typical Phil. She laughed back a sob. Passive aggressive till the end.

The papers that had caught Dani's eye were notes that John McNeil was clearly producing for a book on the history of his family. She'd already seen mentions of Portencross and Seamill amongst the notations in the man's sloping script. This had encouraged her to bring the pile upstairs.

He'd sketched out a family tree that closely resembled the one Ian McNeil had compiled here in Scotland. Dani had Andy's rolled up copy of it leaning against the wall in the corner of her office. She leant across and slipped the document out of its container, laying both items across the desk.

The American's research seemed to go back

further than Ian McNeil's had. His rough diagrams and notes indicated that the family had resided in the West Kilbride area for many generations but before that, had moved down from the Highland

Dani rubbed her eyes as she scanned the births, deaths and marriages listed before her. Her vision lingered on an entry from the late 18th Century, when a branch of the McNeils had bought and established their first boarding house in Portencross. The eldest son of the proprietor, Andrew Duncan McNeil, had married a young woman by the name of Catriona Faulkner in 1793. They had four children between them, who went on to continue the McNeil line for many generations to come.

Dani sat back and crossed her arms over her chest. A member of the Faulkner family had married into the McNeils. John McNeil had discovered this fact.

She looked back at the notes the man had made. Beside this section of the tree John had drawn an arrow leading away from Catriona's name and written, *Faulkner?* To Dani's great surprise, next to this he had scrawled, *any connection to Dale?*

The DCI picked up the phone and dialled. It took a short while before she heard it ring at the other end.

'Hi, Dani? Is everything okay?'

'Sorry if I woke you, Sam.'

'No, I haven't gone to bed yet. Do you wanna talk?'

'I've found John McNeil's notes for his family research.' She explained how the McNeils and the Faulkners had inter-married.

'Okay, so that's our link between the two families. John must have come into contact with Dale because of his genealogy research.'

'Yes, but I think John *already* knew Dale. He's

written the detective's name down in the notes, next to his discovery about Catriona Faulkner. He wrote, *'connection to Dale?'* – as if he knew him, was on first name terms. Is there *any* way John and Dale's paths could have crossed?'

Sam was silent for a moment or two. 'Five years back, Dale did some outreach work in a few of the city schools. His talks were about staying off drugs and out of gangs. Dale was very passionate about it. He may have visited the high school where McNeil taught.'

'Could you look into that for me?'

'Sure, I'll pull up the records first thing tomorrow morning.'

'Thanks.'

'Okay, well, we can talk properly another time, yeah?'

'Yes, I'd like that.'

'Goodnight.'

Chapter 34

Dc Dan Clifton had decided to get a takeout coffee before heading into work. He slipped into one of the tiny cafés along Pitt Street and waited in line.

As he carried his cup towards the main entrance, the detective sensed a presence close behind him. He'd been aware of it in the café too, but only vaguely. He quickened his step before a hand reached out and grabbed his shoulder, causing Dan to curse as hot coffee spilled out over his wrist, scalding the skin.

'Shit!'

'Sorry, detective. Did I make you spill your drink?' The tone wasn't in the least bit sympathetic.

Dan turned and faced his stalker. 'Mrs McRae. You startled me. What are you doing here?'

Nancy McRae was dressed smartly, in a suit and dark green woollen coat. 'I heard that Mr Hemingway has been bribing someone in your department. The officer involved has been thrown off the force.'

'How did you hear that?'

'It was on page two of yesterday's Herald for pity's sake. Hoping to keep it quiet were you?'

'Not at all. It's just that I was going to call and let you know in person, only someone must have leaked it to the press before I had a chance.'

'Someone who doesn't believe that police corruption should be swept under the carpet.' Nancy's expression was steely.

'I wouldn't use the word *corruption*, exactly. It was one individual officer who never touched the money and owned up in the end. I truly don't believe the unfortunate incident had any bearing on the way we investigated your husband's accident.'

'You've got to be kidding me?' Nancy looked incredulous. 'I was coming here today to volunteer my assistance now that you were surely reopening the case.'

Dan's expression was blank. 'There are no plans to do that, Mrs McRae.'

She narrowed her eyes. 'Whose decision is that?'

Dan shrugged his shoulders. He was very intimidated by this woman. 'My boss, DCI Bevan, concluded that there was not enough evidence to pursue an investigation into corporate manslaughter in the death of your husband. But it would be DCS Douglas who took the ultimate decision to halt the process.'

'And neither of those two were taking bribes from Hemingway Shipyards?'

'No! Of course not! That officer is no longer on the police force, I can assure you.'

Nancy threw her arms up in the air. 'But how can you be so sure? If Hemingway had one man in his employ there must be others. You people are so naïve!'

Dan took a step towards her. 'I'm sorry, we did our best. DCI Bevan took the investigation further than our DCS was keen to. She wanted to make the shipyard accountable, but we have to follow the evidence. There wasn't enough to prove that Hemingways breached their duty of care.'

Nancy shook her head sadly. 'I suppose there have to be more deaths before any action is taken. That's what my father always used to say. What does my husband matter in the grand scheme of things? He's just collateral damage.'

Dan didn't quite know how to reply to this. 'I've really got to get to work now.'

'Aye, of course. Your coffee will be getting cold.'

Dan left the woman on the pavement. When he reached his desk on the serious crime floor he went across to look down from the window.

Nancy McRae was still standing there, her vision seemingly fixed on the morning traffic, busily coming and going along Pitt Street.

*

'Great. That's all we need.' Dani perched on the edge of what use to be Phil's desk. 'Someone in the building has leaked the information about Phil's dismissal to the press, *and* we've got Tony McRae's widow on the warpath.'

'It's understandable, Ma'am,' Dan added. 'About Nancy McRae, I mean. You only bribe a member of the police force if you've got something to hide, don't you?'

Dani took a breath. She was struggling to disagree.

'I'm totally on Mrs McRae's side in this,' Andy weighed in, 'but I reckon Raymond Hemingway makes bribery a part of his business plan. It's just his way of dealing with a tricky situation and making it go away. It doesn't actually point to culpability.'

'I think she's going to take it further.' Dan glanced towards the windows, wondering if she was still down there. 'After what happened to her father, and now her husband, I reckon she'll be on some kind of crusade. I wouldn't be surprised if Nancy goes back to the newspapers or even files a civil action against Hemingways.'

'Well, let's hope she does take out a private prosecution against the shipyard. It'll get the woman out of our hair.' Dani addressed her detective constable directly. 'You seem to be the person that Nancy has connected best with, Dan. Make sure you check on her in a few days from now. Let her know we've not forgotten about her or her husband.'

'I won't have anything new to say.' Dan wasn't particularly happy about the prospect of this.

'No, but at least she'll feel we haven't rejected her concerns completely. Mrs McRae may just need a little longer to accept that her husband's death was simply a tragic accident.'

'Fine,' Dan said sulkily. 'I'll drop in on her next week.'

Chapter 35

Dani slid a bottle of wine out of the rack and began opening it. 'Are you okay with a Malbec?'

'Aye, whatever you're having.' Andy examined the notes that his boss had left out on the kitchen table.

'How was Phil when you dropped him off at home?' She found space for their two glasses amongst the files and papers.

'Very subdued. I suppose he was thinking about having to tell Fiona, and then Jane. Note to self, don't get divorced and end up with *two* wives.'

'He'll be okay. Phil was ready to do something new with his life.'

'But they're soon to have all three girls at university. It's not really the best moment to chuck away your career.'

Dani creased her forehead. 'You've got a point there.'

Andy picked up his wine and glanced around him. 'I thought James was due back from Edinburgh this week?'

'He was, but then I got called away to the States and his mum took a turn for the worst.' Dani sipped the wine. 'Linda's got breast cancer, stage three. She had a scare a few years back and the docs thought they'd sorted it. But she found another lump last month.'

'Shit, I'm sorry. What's the prognosis?'

Dani nodded cautiously. 'Good, actually. She's on chemo right now and then they'll operate. Linda is being very brave. I always thought that Jim was the frailer of the two.'

'I suppose James will want to stay with her, the

whole time. I know I would. He can work from over in the east can't he?'

'Yes, he can. There's plenty of room at his parents' place.' She took another slug of Malbec.

'Is there something else?' Andy narrowed his eyes suspiciously.

'Sam Sharpe wants me to marry him – or so he said when we were in Richmond. He's prepared to come and live here in Scotland if I say yes.'

'Bloody hell.' Andy took a few moments to absorb this information. 'I'm certain he's serious. He was asking me about what happened in Norway, during the Maisie Riddell case. He wanted to know why you suddenly changed your mind about the relationship.'

'Did you tell him?' Dani was alarmed.

'No, of course not. You wouldn't give up my secrets and I sure as hell wouldn't give up yours either. I just knew it meant he still had feelings for you. That's all.'

Dani looked him in the eye. 'For the first time in my life, I genuinely don't know what to do, Andy.'

'Do you love James?'

'Yes, but I'm not the person he wants me to be. My lifestyle frustrates him.'

'I don't think that's fair. I've noticed how much you've changed since you've been with him. I'd say you're becoming the person he wants you to be.'

'Is that a good thing? Since being overlooked for the superintendent job, I've just laid down and taken it. It's like I've given up on my ambition.' She flicked her longer, thicker locks. 'I've turned myself into a pretty wee wifie for his benefit.'

'It sounds like you've already made up your mind.' Andy finished his glass, reaching for the bottle to top them both up. 'For what it's worth, I think the guy's made you happier.'

'The last thing Phil said to me was to stop taking

your advice.'

Andy laughed. 'Fair enough.' He tilted his head to one side. 'I suppose my definition of happier is that you're becoming more like my type of lassie – curvier, more homely, with less of an edge – a bit like Carol, in fact. The question is whether or not that's what *you* want. My instinct is that you love them both. Sam has quite possibly come along at the right time. He understands what it's like to live as a cop. If that's what you truly are, then you need to choose him. If you're ready to lessen your role as a police detective and play housie with James, stick with the status quo.'

'I've reached a cross-roads, is that what you're saying?'

'Aye, I probably am. But then my advice isn't worth shit, apparently.'

Dani chuckled. 'Actually, I think you've hit the nail on the head.'

Andy glanced down at the papers spread between them, sensing it was time to change the subject. 'So the Faulkner family were related to the McNeils?

'Yes, if we put together John's research with Ian's we get pretty much the full picture. It was the descendants of Andrew and Catriona who ended up emigrating to the United States in the 1840s.'

'So John McNeil and Dale Faulkner were related?'

'Only in an incredibly distant way. They might have shared great-great-great grandparents, that's all.'

'But this would have been an exciting discovery for someone like John, who spent a lot of his time researching the family heritage.'

Dani's phone began to ring. 'Hi, Sam. Have you got something for me? Hang on, Andy's here. I'll put you on speakerphone.'

'Hi Andy, how's it going?'

'Good, aye. Dani's just filling me in on the John McNeil angle.'

'Well, I may have some information to add. I spoke with McNeil's principal again. According to the school records, Dale visited the high school on three occasions between May 2010 and June 2011. During those years, John was the head of student welfare for the middle grades. The principal was convinced that John would have coordinated the talks that Dale gave to the students.'

'So that's how they met.'

'The current principal only started the job in 2013. He pieced this together from the computer system. The link was there all along. We just needed to ask the right questions. I'm sorry I didn't recall the outreach work Dale did earlier. It was something that he volunteered for. He gave those talks pretty much in his own time. I'd almost forgotten he'd ever done it.'

'Well, we know the connection between the two men now,' Dani replied levelly. 'They must have met in 2009, when Dale came to speak to John's students about drugs and gang culture. I wonder what drew them to one another.'

'They were related,' Andy chipped in. 'However distantly, and that can create a sense of affinity. I had a great pal back at training college who it turned out was one of my second cousins. Neither of us had the slightest idea. I know it isn't scientific, but I reckon we had enough shared characteristics to be drawn to each other as friends.'

Dani was sceptical about this theory, but she didn't contradict him. 'The relationship between Dale and John may only have been fleeting, simply two professionals whose paths crossed at the high school occasionally. Then, when John was completing his genealogy research, the name Faulkner happened to come up.'

'He decided to look Dale up again, to ask his family were also from Portencross in Ayrshire,' Sam continued.

'Dale didn't want that particular connectic to become public knowledge,' Dani said steadily 'He hadn't even told his own wife and children abou his childhood, let alone some guy he barely knew who happened to be constructing a family tree.'

'Not just a family tree,' Andy pitched in. 'M ybe he told Dale there was going to be a book to - a whole entire history of the McNeils and the Faulkners, available for sale in the booksho of Richmond.'

The crackly line was silent for several mom nts. Dani worried they may have lost the conne ion.

Finally Sam said, 'Then maybe John told Da he and Rita were heading back to West Kilbride t live out their retirement, to finally put all the piec s of the family puzzle together, to complete his ook where the story had first begun.' He sighed he vily. 'I've got a bad feeling about where this investig tion is leading us. A *really* bad feeling.'

Chapter 36

Sam Sharpe experienced a restless night. When he was on the hands-free to Dani he hadn't sensed there was anyone at her place except Calder. But he had no idea what that meant and still didn't have a clue which way she was going to jump.

As soon as it became light, Sam padded into the kitchen of his one-bedroom, city centre apartment and started to make coffee. The other cause of his sleeplessness was the doubt forming in his mind about his old friend Dale.

Up until now, he'd assumed that whoever killed the McNeils, stuffed their brutalized bodies in a freezer box and then buried them in the yard of that run-down old house on the Southside, had also shot Dale. His cop's instinct wasn't telling him that any longer.

Sam took a shower and pulled on his jeans and a casual sweater. He drove out to Midlothian, sitting in his SUV and watching Toni Faulkner pottering around in the kitchen for a while. Finally, the detective opened up and approached the front door.

Toni looked surprised to see him. She ran a hand through her loose hair. 'Hi, Sam, I wasn't expecting you this morning.'

'No, I didn't call ahead. Sorry.'

'Not a problem, you're welcome anytime.' She stood back and allowed him to enter. Toni led her visitor into the kitchen and began filling the coffee machine. 'I'm clean out of pods.'

'Coffee from a machine is just fine.' He sat on a stool at the breakfast bar.

'Is that lady detective not will you this time?' Toni

avoided eye contact, keeping herself busy opening a fresh packet of ground beans.

'Dani's gone back to Scotland.'

'Only I recalled, after you'd gone the other day, how you'd had a girlfriend who was in the police over in Glasgow, a while back.'

'Yeah, that was her.'

Toni's shoulders seemed to drop just a fraction. 'She seemed nice. Good at her job.'

'She is. Look, I didn't come here to discuss my dating history.'

Toni turned round, her forehead wrinkling into a frown. 'Have you found something out about Dale's murder?'

'Kind've.' Sam stood up and moved closer. 'I know it's tough, but I need you to tell me about the period of time between two years and eighteen months ago. When Dale ended your marriage.'

'What do you want to know?' Toni turned her back on the detective.

'How was he behaving? Did he say or do anything out of the ordinary during that period?'

Toni shrugged. 'Apart from ending a twenty year marriage I thought was perfectly happy, you mean?'

Sam allowed her to formulate a proper answer, carrying their cups over to the breakfast bar and sitting there patiently, pretending to enjoy the coffee.

'He'd been working long hours on that drug case – the one that took you out to Virginia Beach at the time.'

Sam nodded, he remembered it well.

'Only as a detective's wife you've gotta take a lot of stuff on trust, you know? He's out until the early hours and when he comes back, he claims it was work. What can you do? You've gotta believe him.'

'That case did take up a great deal of man hours. I should know. I filed the overtime sheets.'

Toni managed a thin smile. 'I didn't see a whole lot of Dale in the month or so before he left. In fact, the kids and I went away to my parents' cabin in the Blue Ridge for a couple of weeks. Dale was real busy on the case and couldn't join us.'

'When was this exactly?' Sam carefully put down his cup.

'It was the summer of 2014. I'd have to find my old calendar to get the exact date.'

'While you were away, Dale remained here, in the house?'

'Yeah, he hadn't moved out yet. He dropped his bombshell not long after we returned from that vacation. It must have been in the early September. But Dale hadn't been himself that whole summer. He was real distant and wouldn't talk to me, not properly.'

'Was there a part of the house that Dale used to hang out in – like a workshop or a den, maybe?'

'Dale wasn't a great one for making things, but he stored all his gardening gear in the basement. It's where we keep the bikes. He used to go down and work on those occasionally, fixing punctures and adjusting stuff.'

'Do you mind if I take a look in there?'

'Sure, although it's a mess. No one's used it since Dale went. The kids got new bikes for college.'

Toni lifted a key off a hook by the large refrigerator and unlocked the door under the stairs. She flicked a light switch and stood back. 'Go ahead, but watch your footing, there may be boxes on the steps.'

Sam descended cautiously. The overhead bulb wasn't throwing out much light and he was struggling to get accustomed to the gloom.

The large space beneath the Faulkners' home was filled with the usual detritus of family life. The bikes were leaning against one of the wooden support struts and a workbench stood in one corner. Sam manoeuvred through the piles of camping gear, peering under dusty sheets and shifting old blankets aside in the process.

Then something caught the detective's eye. One corner of the basement seemed to have been allocated to the storage of the Faulkners' luggage. Sam moved across to examine the cases and trunks, each of them bearing flight labels for various destinations; Florida, New York, Washington DC

But one pair of suitcases didn't quite match the rest. They were more old-fashioned and were of the kind that Sam's own parents tended to use. He dragged one of them forward and undid the zips. The case itself was empty. Sam ran his fingers around the interior, searching for any pockets in which something may have been missed. Nothing.

He pulled over the second suitcase. This one was slightly smaller than the first. Again, Sam folded back the lid and examined the interior. Instantly his hand shot forward and touched a small, hand-sewn label which had been woven into the lining of the base, its material so closely matching the upholstery of the case that on first glance you could easily miss it.

The label read: Mrs R.E. McNeil. Richmond, Virginia. U.S.A.

Chapter 37

Dani addressed her team in the conference room of the Pitt Street HQ.

'We've been looking at this investigation from the wrong angle,' she began, eyeing each detective in turn. 'Now we have the McNeils' suitcases, recovered from the basement of the Faulkner property in Richmond, it changes everything.'

'Dale Faulkner murdered the McNeils in the summer of 2014. *He* placed their bodies in the freezer of their rented property,' Alice supplied.

'It seems increasingly likely that is what happened. Toni Faulkner and the children spent two weeks at her parents' cabin that summer; from the 12th to the 26th of July. Dale may have killed the couple before this date and used the absence of his wife from their property to dispose of the bodies and clean up the crime scene.'

'But *why* would Dale do something like that?' Dan looked genuinely crestfallen. 'He was a friend of Detective Sharpe's. They'd known each other for decades.'

Andy got to his feet. 'Dale Faulkner wasn't the guy people thought he was. He'd lied to his wife and children from day one. The man was hiding something terrible from his past. He bludgeoned to death a harmless old couple in order to keep it a secret.'

Dani shook her head in frustration. 'We should have known that whoever killed the McNeils had a good knowledge of forensics. He stored the bodies in the freezer until he had an opportunity to bury them. Dale was determined to cover his tracks.'

'So who made the 911 callout to the property where the McNeils' were buried and shot Dale in the head?' Alice Mann asked bluntly.

'Someone must have discovered what Dale had done,' Dani continued. 'Perhaps they'd contacted Dale before the night of his death and that's why he decided to bury the bodies after all that time.'

'Could this person have been blackmailing him?' Andy pitched in.

'It's certainly possible. But then why kill him? They'd lose their supply of cash with Dale dead.' Dani ran a hand through her hair.

'How does this tie in with the murder of Vicki Kendrick?' Alice wanted to steer the discussion back to their Glasgow investigation.

'Well, I think they both knew the secret – Dale and Vicki.' Dani tapped her finger on their photographs, pinned up side-by-side. 'Somebody wanted them both to pay for their sins. *That's* who we're looking for.'

'It seems like Dale had committed quite a few of those,' Andy said with distaste. 'How is Sam taking the news?'

'Perfectly professionally, as far as I can tell. The Richmond PD are tearing apart the Faulkners' home right now, looking for more evidence. What they have as it stands is purely circumstantial. We don't know where Dale dumped the murder weapon or the contents of the suitcases. They may have gone into the James River somewhere. It's unlikely they'll be recovered after all this time.'

'Keeping the suitcases themselves was a gamble,' Alice commented.

'Perhaps they were just too big to dispose of. Dale thought he'd removed all traces of the McNeils from them. He may even have told Toni they'd once belonged to his parents and he'd inherited them. She wouldn't have questioned it. Dale was a policeman. He knew nobody was actually searching for the McNeils. They had no children and no immediate family in the area. The couple told everyone they knew in Richmond that they were about to go off travelling. They hadn't been missed. If Dale himself hadn't been murdered in that house and the landlord forced to refurbish the place, we may never have discovered what happened to them at all.'

Andy's face had flushed red with anger. 'I don't think we should feel sentimental about this guy, Dale. We need to forget all about the fact he was a cop, like us. I say we dig over that family's history until we find the dirty little secret they were all hiding. Then we blow it sky high.'

Dani nodded. 'Don't worry DS Calder. That is my intention exactly.'

Chapter 38

As soon as Dani opened the door to her flat she sensed something was wrong. It immed tely occurred to her that James might have retu ned from Edinburgh.

She placed her briefcase in the hall and mad her way towards the kitchen, calling out her boyfri 1d's name but without switching on the lights. The first thing she noticed was that the lock on her patio loor had been broken. It was wrenched open just en ugh for someone to have squeezed inside.

Dani glanced around her, the hairs on the ack of her neck standing on end. There was no oise except for the humming of the fridge. She pa ded towards the bedroom, careful not to touch anyt ing. Bracing herself, Dani kicked open the door wit her foot. The room was empty.

She turned and gazed into the gloom o the sitting room. At first, everything appeared to e in order. Then Dani noticed several dark streaks a oss the walls and floor. Pulling her sleeve down ove her hand she flicked on the light switch.

There were glass fragments all over the offee table and sofa. It took Dani several minutes to ork out that the stains on the paintwork were rom several bottles of red wine now smashed into p ces and strewn across the furniture. Someone had broken into her flat, emptied out her wine rack and gone to town with the contents all over the ont room.

Dani felt the phone in her pocket start to uzz. She lifted it out. It was Andy.

'Hi.'

'Evening, Ma'am. Sorry to bother you at this time. There's been an odd incident.'

'Ditto.'

'Huh?'

'Carry on, you first.'

'DCS Douglas arrived home to find his wife's car had been vandalised. It's been scratched with what appears to be a broken bottle. The words, 'filthy scab,' were gouged across the side of the paintwork.'

'I think the broken bottle came from my kitchen.'

'*What?*'

'I'll need a forensic team over to my place straight away. As soon as I've had my back door secured by the locksmith, I'll come and join you at headquarters.'

*

The only detectives still on duty were Andy, Alice and Dan. Bevan called them all into her office.

'The DCS decided to stay at home to comfort his wife. She's very upset at the thought of some nutter having a go at her new car. She's worried it might be personal.' Andy reclined comfortably on the sofa.

Dani shook her head. 'It isn't. This person was targeting me and the DCS. It just happened to be Alison's car parked on the driveway.'

'The Douglas place is like Fort Knox. All the doors are wired up to some kind of central alarm system. Plus the wife was at home for most of the day, just popping in and out for provisions. I reckon this vandal didn't fancy their chances of getting inside the place undetected.'

'Maybe I'd better update my home security,' Dani added bitterly.

'The techies have gone through your place lifting prints. They told me a new lock's been fitted to your back door, a much better model. The old one couldn't take much jemmying to snap it in two.' Andy was clearly making an attempt to be reassuring.

'Why were the DCS and I targeted? I know that we're pretty unpopular with a good number of Glasgow's villains, but why the both of us and why now?'

Dan Clifton cleared his throat nervously. 'When I got approached by Nancy McRae the other morning, she was really upset about the idea that the police had taken bribes from Hemingway. I felt I had to provide her with as full an explanation as possible as to why we closed down the case into her husband's death.'

Dani narrowed her eyes. 'What did you tell her?'

'She wanted to know exactly whose decision it was to stop the investigation. I said that it was you and the DCS who decided there was no negligence case to answer.'

Andy turned on his colleague. 'Why the hell did you tell her that?'

'She was angry that we weren't reopening the file, despite the fact that an officer had been dismissed for taking a bribe from the shipyard. I felt I owed her a better explanation.'

Dani placed both hands in the air. 'At least we now have something to go on.'

Andy made a face. 'Do we really think that Tony McRae's widow broke into your flat, Ma'am?'

Dan Clifton shuffled forward in his chair. 'The words scrawled on Mrs Douglas's car were, '*lthy scab*'. That's an insult that used to be hurled at workers who broke a strike – folk who were seen to have betrayed the union. Nancy McRae hails from that background. Her father was Alec Duff. Even if *she* didn't carry out the vandalism, I'm certain Nancy would know of somebody who would do it for her.

The Duffs were urban heroes in certain Glasgow circles in the 70s and 80s.'

'Right, you and Andy head out first thing in the morning to have a wee chat with Mrs McRae. If she can't give us a watertight alibi for what she was up to this afternoon, bring her in for a formal interview.'

Chapter 39

It was the first time Andy had met Tony Mc ae's widow. Although in her early fifties, the womar had a youthful and athletic appearance. The only si n of her age was the greying of her otherwise thick, lark hair at the fringe.

Nancy opened the door to the officers w h a smile. 'Ah, DC Clifton. Come inside, please.'

Andy pulled out his ID card and introc ced himself.

Their host was already preparing them drin s. 'I know that the young DC takes coffee. How & out you, love?'

'I'll have the same,' Andy replied, suddenly fe ling distinctly awkward about the nature of their visi

Nancy entered the front room a few mon nts later with their cups on a tray. 'I'm glad y u've dropped by.' She placed the load down and o red around the milk and sugar. 'I felt awful about how I'd ambushed you in the street the other day DC Clifton. It was just that reading that article in the paper about Hemingway's Shipyard had mad me extremely upset. But I shouldn't have taken it o t on you, I'm sorry.'

Dan mumbled some dismissive words int his coffee.

Andy sat up straight, puffing out his chest. Mrs McRae. There was an incident yesterday, in v ich two of our most senior officers experienced se ous acts of vandalism on their property. DC C fton informed us that he told you these two officers vere responsible for halting the investigation into our husband's accident. Do you know anything & out these attacks?'

Nancy looked genuinely shocked. 'Good Lord, no. What on earth would such a mindless act of destruction achieve?'

'Where were you yesterday afternoon, Ma'am?'

She put the coffee cup to her lips and considered this. 'I had lunch with an old friend of the family, Finnian Blake. I must have left the restaurant at two, because I had a meeting to attend at Govan Town Hall at three. I've established a new group, for the widows and widowers of workers killed in industrial accidents. For a first meeting, it was very well attended. I spoke for forty five minutes. Then there was a lively question and answer session. I must have been at the hall until nearly seven o'clock. One of the committee members drove me home. I can supply you with their number, if you'd like?'

'Yes please, that would be helpful.' Andy took a breath. 'Might you have mentioned to someone that DCI Bevan and DCS Douglas were responsible for putting Hemingway Shipyards in the clear over the death of your husband?'

'Well, I didn't think the information was confidential, as DC Clifton had told me it in the street. As a matter of fact, I put it in my speech yesterday. There were a few hundred folk present in the hall and a handful of representatives from the local press. I expect it was all over the social media sites within minutes of the words leaving my mouth.'

*

'Is she deliberately trying to piss us off?' Dani paced across the tiny amount of floor space available in her office.

'She's a formidable woman to get on the wrong

side of,' Andy offered. 'She grew up amongst act ists and union heavy weights. I expect Nancy M Rae knows how to make waves without actually ( )ing something illegal. It's going to be very difficult t pin down who may have committed the attacks or you and the DCS now. The suspect list has expand d to include about half of Glasgow.'

'There were no prints left in either case. The perps must have been wearing gloves.' Dani s hed and gazed up at the ceiling. 'I wonder how r uch trouble this woman is intending to cause?'

'I think her real beef is with the shipyard, M am. I was checking her alibi when we got back this morning. Nancy said she was having lunch wit an old family friend yesterday. It was Finnian E ike. He's a solicitor who specialises in cases of corp rate negligence. Over the years, his firm has take on some of Scotland's business giants.'

'So Nancy is planning on initiating a privat(suit against Hemingways? Good. That should shif her attention away from us.'

Andy eyed his boss carefully. 'Did you go ack home last night? You know you're welcome to stay with me and Carol for a few days, until the fla gets properly cleaned up?'

Dani stopped pacing. 'Actually, I staye in Rhodri's spare room. I'm going to be at his plac for the rest of this week.'

'Okay, good. Did you tell James about the b ak-in?'

Dani shook her head. 'No, he's got enough tc leal with right now. I've got a cleaning company co ing in today. It looks like I might have to re-pain the walls in the sitting room. After that, there no reason why James needs to know what happene .'

'I think he'd *want* to know.'

'If I tell him, Andy, then he'll come ru ing

straight back. That's the last thing I want him to do right now.'

'Fine, it's your call. But while you're at Rhodri's place, get his opinion on the Faulkner case. You might as well pick his brains, without the psychologist's fees ending up on our investigation budget.'

Dani laughed. 'Every cloud has a silver lining, eh?'

'Well, you said it Ma'am, not me.'

Chapter 40

Professor Rhodri Morgan settled back into his armchair with a glass of single malt cradled in his lap. 'Are you sure you've had enough to eat?'

'Aye, thank you. I'm not really used to having a proper meal during the week. Not since James has been gone, anyway.'

'When is he returning to Glasgow?' Rhodri peered at his younger friend over the top of his glasses, those bright blue eyes examining her response carefully.

'His mum needs him right now. Her treatment is going to be tough and could last several months.'

'This may sound brutal, but James also has to look to his own future. He will have to balance the care for his mother alongside his relationship with you. It is an age-old dilemma.'

'I don't mind, I've been busy at work.' Dani slowly sipped her whisky.

Rhodri knitted his brow. 'Do you *want* him to come back?'

Dani sighed heavily and told the professor about Sam Sharpe's proposal.

'Ah, yet another age-old dilemma. I sensed here was something wrong.'

'I don't suppose you could tell me what I should do?'

Rhodri chuckled. 'No, but I can tell you a story, about a man who was madly in love with a woman who was already married with a young child. He knew she wasn't happy with her husband but loved the child and was terrified of losing her. The man proposed, offering to take the child on as his own.

The woman feared the child would choose to stay with her real father, so she turned him down.'

'It's the story of you and my mum.' Dani felt her eyes start to glisten with tears. She took another gulp of the whisky. 'You went on to live a good life.'

'Oh yes, I made the best of it, as all of us do. But I lost the only woman I truly loved.'

'You're saying I need to choose the person I truly love. Only I genuinely don't know who that is. I love them both, Rhodri.'

He shrugged his shoulders. 'I believe you will know when the time comes. You probably already do, but your desire to 'do the right thing' is colouring your judgement. All I am saying is that doing the right thing can be terribly over-rated.' He formed a sad smile.

Dani smiled back and raised her glass. 'I'll drink to that.'

*

When DCS Douglas strode across the floor of the serious crime division, he looked flustered. Dani sprang out from behind her desk to open the door for him.

'Good morning, sir. How is Mrs Douglas?'

'Gradually calming down. A replacement vehicle has arrived, whilst the repairs are done. Thankfully, the whole sorry incident has been covered by our insurance.' He cleared his throat, suddenly realising that perhaps Dani's experience had been a tad worse. 'How about your flat? Everything sorted there?'

'The decorators have been in, thanks. There wasn't a great deal of damage done. But it's the thought of someone being in your home, sir.'

Douglas ran a hand through his thick, silvery

hair. 'Yes, it is. That's why Alison's been so shaken up, I think. It's the malicious intent rather than the damned car. And the words that were written on the side were oddly disturbing.'

'Like a throwback to a bygone era, when clashes between strikers and the police was commonplace. There was definitely a 'them and us' situation back then.'

'Which I was keen to believe was well behind us.' The DCS took a chair. 'My father was a sergeant during the steelworkers' strikes of the early seventies. He faced down a number of picket lines in those days. It was a tough time for him and my mother. I recall the terrible strain it put on them. He was spat at in the street once, when he was off duty and taking me to the football. I'll never forget it. Do you think that's why I was targeted?'

Dani shook her head. 'No, I'm certain it was because Nancy McRae released our names to her pressure group and the press. Some lunatics picked up on the fact we'd allowed Hemingways off the hook. I don't expect they'd have the gumption to look too deeply into the history of either of us. They were perhaps members of an anti-capitalist organisation. DS Mann is looking into it.'

Douglas appeared relieved.

'Did your father ever mention Alec Duff?'

'The union boss? He didn't have to. The guy was everywhere – on the news, the front of the red tops. He was a working class hero.'

Dani frowned with concentration. 'I find it odd that Nancy Duff would have married a man like Tony McRae. I sense he didn't possess the strength of conviction that his wife did. Don't women usually seek out men who are like their fathers?'

'Perhaps McRae wasn't her first choice. It would have been a hard act to follow anyway. They broke the mould after they made Alec Duff.'

'How did the Glasgow police view his death?'

'Well, no one condoned the man's murder, of course. But privately, my father was relieved Duff was gone. His presence made it difficult for any compromises to be reached between the two sides. He was the great symbol of union power along the Clyde. When he'd gone it was easier for the workers to recognise that change was inevitable.'

'Or be broken, whichever way you happened to view it.'

'Aye, that's true enough. But you're too young to remember, Danielle. *Everybody* suffered during those strikes - the families of the strikers probably worse than most. Many had to rely on handouts to feed their weans.'

'But the union leaders themselves sometimes profited?' Dani recalled her own father complaining about this fact at the time.

Douglas waggled his finger. 'Now that's dangerous talk, DCI Bevan. Don't let it be heard outside these walls.'

'It might explain why Duff was murdered by one of his own, though.'

'The situation was complicated. The man who shot Duff was desperate. It wasn't the grand conspiracy that some folk at the time painted it to be.'

Dani nodded. Like Phil's fall from grace, these incidents were usually a combination of a misunderstanding plus a feeling of being pushed to the edge. But the DCS had given her plenty to think about. His words had brought to mind something that Andy had mentioned before about the Faulkner case.

Chapter 41

As the long winter finally seemed to be fading into a bright, mild spring, Dani walked along the beach at Portencross and watched the waves breaking onto the shore.

She heard the shingle being churned under foot as Andy jogged to catch her up. 'Did you get a decent night's sleep?'

'Yes, thanks. The hotel is pretty basic, but there was a fabulous view.'

'You must have had the same room Sam did.'

'What have you found out?'

'There was a record of Mr and Mrs Faulkner of Crosbie Farm providing food parcels for some of the striking families of South Glasgow. They contained fresh fruit and vegetables, eggs and milk. The steelworkers' union archivist provided me with a list of names. Some of the contributions came from as far away as Pittsburgh in the US. They sent pretty diverse stuff too - from tinned goods to clothes and shoes.'

'Never underestimate the sense of solidarity that exists between people in the same profession. Look at us coppers. We're as bad.'

Dani stared at the distant outline of the Arran hills before saying, 'why did the Faulkners give handouts to the strikers? It doesn't sound as if they had a great deal to spare themselves. What was their connection to the workers on the Clyde?'

Andy raised his eyebrows and gave a grin. 'Remember that Magnus Faulkner had two brothers? The younger one, whose death was recorded in the early eighties, was called Joseph Faulkner. He worked for the Ferris and Brewer Shipyard. More than that, he was a shop steward - a union rep for the MWSDU.'

'The same union that Alec Duff worked for?'

'Aye. So the Faulkners *did* have a connection to the strikes. That's obviously why they wanted to contribute.'

'Let's find somewhere warmer to talk this through.'

They walked towards the castle, where a small café had been erected in a pre-fab near the carpark. Andy bought them both a coffee.

'What happened to Joseph Faulkner?' Dani emptied a couple of sugars into her drink, sensing it wouldn't be drinkable without some enhancement.

'I got Alice to dig out his death certificate. He was declared dead in 1981, when he would have been forty two years old. In fact he'd gone missing, in the December of 1974. Last seen in one of the seedier pubs of Govan, three sheets to the wind. The police report suggested he most likely got his throat slit by robbers and ended up in the Clyde.'

Dani's mind drifted to the photograph she'd held in Dale Faulkner's apartment in Richmond. It was a family Christmas scene with Dale, Vicki and their parents at the farmhouse kitchen table plus a couple of dark-haired, handsome men who she'd taken for Magnus's brothers. She couldn't quite recall the date written on the back. 'And a body was never found?'

'Nope.' Andy grimaced as he downed the dregs of his cup. '*Jesus*, that was bad.'

'I want to go to Crosbie Farm.' Dani stood up, sprinkling a selection of change on the Formica table top.

'It doesn't exist any longer, Ma'am. There's a bloody great housing estate built on top of it.'

'Then take me to the housing estate. I want to see

what it's like.'

Andy drove and Dani sat beside him in silence. The estate seemed to rise out of nowhere, nestled in a valley that was surrounded on all sides by gentle, rolling hills. The houses were nicely designed, using the local sandstone to help them blend into the landscape.

But still, Dani didn't like this place.

Andy parked up near the show homes and sales office. 'This is as close as we can get to where the farmhouse once stood.'

They got out of the car. Dani gazed around her. 'When did the Faulkners move to America?' She knew the answer to this, but wanted Andy to help her go over the evidence again.

'They left Scotland on the 25th July 1976.'

'That was roughly eighteen months after Joseph Faulkner went missing.'

'Do you think the events are connected?'

'Yes, I'm beginning to. Did Joseph have a wife, any children?'

'No, he hadn't ever been married.'

'So he had no one to spend Christmas with except his middle brother and family, here at Crosbie Farm.' As Dani scanned the lush fields, an image formed in her mind. It was a date, written in biro on Kodak paper, faded with age.

December 1974.

She turned to face her friend. 'I've seen a photo of them together. Dale kept it all those years. It was in his apartment when Sam and I searched it.'

'There must have been plenty of family shots; it's no surprise Dale wanted one for a keepsake.' Andy looked puzzled.

Dani shook her head vigorously. 'No, it was taken *that* Christmas, in the December of '74, over the period when Joseph went missing. What if he was at

Crosbie Farm *after* the night he spent at the pub in Govan? He had nobody at home to vouch for his whereabouts.'

'Then the Faulkner family would have reported it to the police, wouldn't they?'

'What if they didn't? It might have suited Magnus for the police to believe that his wee brother fell foul of some Southside ne'er do wells picking on drunken Christmas revellers. He may have wanted people to think Joseph ended up in the river with his throat slit.'

'If the last place Joseph was ever seen was actually here, at Crosbie Farm, then what really happened to him?'

'Come on,' Dani pulled open the car door. 'We need to get back to Glasgow. The answer lies there, I'm certain of it.'

Chapter 42

Detective Sharpe was beginning to get a little tired of women crying on his shoulder. First, he had to deal with the disgust and disbelief of Toni Faulkner. Now Cassie Sanchez was threatening to fall to pieces in front of him.

'Take a seat, Cassie. I'll send Pete out for some coffees.'

The tears had started to slide down her smooth cheeks. 'I just can't get my head around it, boss. I read the medical examiner's report. I saw the photos. Both the McNeils' skulls had been caved in by a blunt object. Their bones had to be broken in order to stuff them into that refrigerator.' The detective made a gagging sound. Sam thought she might vomit.

'You need to go home, Cassie. Take a few days off. Fly down to visit your folks if necessary. I don't mind. Forget about Dale Faulkner. We were all taken in. The guy must have been desperate to do what he did to those old folks, but even that's not enough to explain the horror of it.'

An overweight man in uniform placed a tall stout coffee cup directly into Cassie Sanchez's shaking hand. 'Drink up sweetheart. I put plenty of sugars in there.'

The woman did as instructed and seemed to calm down a little. 'I will take some time off, thanks.'

Sam leant forward. 'You've had a lucky escape. You might have married the son-of-a-bitch without ever knowing what he was capable of. Look at poor Toni. She had three kids with the bastard. Go off and live the rest of your life, Cassie, and never for one goddam minute look back.'

She nodded. Clearly recognising this as good advice, Sanchez lifted her jacket with one hand and with her coffee in the other, walked slowly towards the door, giving her boss a shaky salute on the way out.

Sam turned his attention back to the file on his desk. He'd barely had more than a couple of hours sleep in a row since he discovered the McNeils' suitcases in Dale's basement. Since then, he'd scoured his old friend's case files, diaries and appointments going back as far as when he first joined the Richmond PD.

So far, Sam hadn't discovered any anomalies. Dale had spent time in the traffic department and in narcotics before joining the homicide division. The detective had a good clear-up rate and was well regarded by his superiors. Dale had experienced his longest stint as a detective dealing with drug law enforcement. Sam picked up the phone and dialled the number of a captain he knew on that floor.

'Hi, David, it's Sharpe here, from Homicide.'

'Hey, Sam. What can I do for you? Got a drug-related shooting for me?'

'Not today. I'm interested in talking about Dale Faulkner. He worked for you guys for a while, is that right?'

The man sighed. 'Yeah, he did. One of my best officers, too. I can't believe what they're saying he did to those two old folks.'

'You've heard then?'

David chuckled. 'You can't keep anything quiet in a cop shop.'

'I've looked through the cases Dale handled. He had a very good clear-up rate. Dale got involved in the prevention side too, didn't he? Giving talks to high school kids, that kind of thing?'

'Yep, that's right. Dale actually understood that we were getting to these situations too late. Once the kids were hooked on crack they got sucked into street crime and couldn't get out again. He got frustrated just mopping up the mess left behind'

'That type of citizenship doesn't really fit with a man capable of a violent homicide.'

'No, but Dale had some kind of personal experience of the damaging effects of drugs. That's why he asked to get placed in my unit.'

'In what way?' Sam shuffled up straighter in his seat.

'I dunno the details really. He told me about it a long time ago. There was a young girl he knew back on his folks' farm. She was the girlfriend of his cousin, or somethin' like that. The cousin went way and left her and this young girl couldn't get over it. She started shooting up heroin and hanging about the Faulkners' place making trouble. He said they tried to help her but she was beyond anything they could do by then.'

'What happened to this girl?'

'He never said. But they usually get picked up by a local pimp, start working the streets to support their habit. It's a sad story, but not an unusual one.'

'Thanks David, you've been a great help.'

'Sure, no problem.' The man cleared his throat. 'I know Dale did somethin' real bad, but I'm trying to focus on the good stuff he did, you know?'

'Yeah, me too,' Sam replied quietly, but he wasn't really listening any more, his mind was busy running through the information he'd just heard

Chapter 43

Dani had spent a few hours tracking down the files relating to the disappearance of Joseph Faulkner in 1974. She had her whole team carefully scanning through the details.

'I wonder if the SIO on the case is still alive?'

Andy turned to his computer screen. 'What's the name, I can try the database?'

Dani glanced back down at the pile of papers in front of her. 'DI Maider, Francis P..'

Andy tapped away for a few minutes. 'Frank Maider, retired in 1995. There's no record of his death.'

'See if you can find out where he is now, would you Andy?'

'Sure.'

Dani looked again at her notes. 'Joseph Faulkner, known as Joe, was a sheet metal worker by trade. He was thirty five years old when he went missing. Judging by the photos in the file, he was dark in colouring and good looking. I'd be amazed if there wasn't a girlfriend somewhere.'

'Several witness statements were taken from the Kingston Bar on Govan Road where he was last seen.' Andy flicked back a few pages. 'On the 19th December 1974.'

'Joe had digs near the Southern General Hospital. The police never worked out whether he reached home or not that evening. He had plenty of belongings and his passport in the flat. But his wallet was missing along with him.'

'Did Joe have a car?'

Dani turned over several sheets. 'It doesn't seem

so. His digs were near enough to the Ferris Brewer yard for him not to need one.'

Andy looked up from the page. 'If he travelled to the Faulkner place in Portencross, after the time he was last sighted, how did he get there?'

Dani considered this. 'Where did the other brother live – the older one?'

'Keith Faulkner?' Andy had to fish out his notebook for this information. 'He died in a nursing home in Kilmarnock in 2013. I've no history of his former addresses, but I can find out.'

'Can you do that? For now, I think we can assume Keith was in the Glasgow area in '74. There were three brothers in that Christmas photograph I saw. Maybe Keith gave his brother a lift down to Magnus's place?'

Andy nodded. 'It makes sense.'

Dani rested her head in her hand. 'Joe Faulkner was working at the Ferris Brewer Shipyard in 1974. He was a shop steward and must have been involved in the industrial disputes which went on during that time. Do you remember what it was like back then?'

'I was only a bairn. But the people Sam and I interviewed in Portencross and Seamill spoke about it. Most workers were on a three-day week. They said the rolling power cuts were the worst. I remember my Ma talking about sitting in a hairdressers in the semi-darkness, her sopping wet hair dripping down the back of her neck, waiting for the electricity to come back on.'

Dani looked up some information on her smartphone. 'There were shortages of certain goods. People were panic buying candles for the power cuts. Folk had to boil kettles on open coal fires to get hot water. It sounds like a terrible time to be living through, like a war was going on or something.'

'It *was* a type of war, I suppose - between the

unions and their bosses.'

'The old world and the new having a showdown.' Dani crinkled her brow. 'Magnus Faulkner and his wife provided food parcels for strikers at the steelworks on the Clyde. We assumed they did this because of their link to Joe. But it must have been a strain. They would have been struggling to support themselves during that tough time, let alone providing handouts to others.'

'Perhaps Joe was pressurising his brother into contributing. Maybe Magnus finally had enough. It wasn't *his* cause, after all.'

'The situation reached a head that Christmas. Magnus told his brother that he couldn't support the steelworkers any longer. He was going to concentrate on his own family from that point onwards.'

'Joe was hot-headed, dedicated to his men and to keeping the ship-building industry in Scotland alive. The two men fought. Magnus may have been defending himself.'

'But either way, Joe wound up dead. They got rid of his body and denied ever seeing him.'

'Were the whole family involved? Even the wife, the kids?'

'They must have been. Perhaps they saw what happened, were caught up in the argument, maybe even the violence.'

Andy shrugged his shoulders in frustration. 'This is just conjecture, wild theories. We've got absolutely no way of finding out the truth. All the possible witnesses are now dead.' He counted them off on his fingers. 'Magnus, Sue, Keith, Maeve, Dale and even Vicki – all gone.'

'But maybe there's still one more person who knows what happened. Another witness. The one who's searching for justice, coming back to make sure the others pay for what they did. That's who we need to find.'

Chapter 44

Sam's flight had landed in the early hours of morning. He couldn't check into his hotel until much later in the day, but he didn't plan on wasting the time.

After speaking with David in Narcotics, Sam went back to his notes. He was certain that when Dale had talked about a young girl hanging around his parents' farm, he was meaning Crosbie Farm in Scotland, not their place in Virginia.

Sam decided that Dale's secret must have something to do with her. Perhaps she overdosed at the property and the Faulkners were unable to save her? Sam didn't know for certain, but he felt he had a strong lead with this information.

If the incident happened before the Faulkners took off for the States, then he was looking at the early seventies. Sam's first port of call was to check out all the drug hostels and rehabilitation centres in Glasgow. It was a long shot that they would have records going back as far as forty years, but he didn't have anywhere else to start. It was a needle in a haystack sort of task. But then Sam quite liked those.

The American detective had already compiled a list of numbers and addresses on the plane. He zipped his jacket up tight to the neck and headed towards the centre of town.

*

Andy walked up to the door of the porter's lodge and

rang the bell.

After a short wait, a woman slid back a p stic screen and peered out. 'Who are you here to see, love?'

'Frank Maider, number 16.' Andy held up his ID.

'Fine, go straight ahead and to the left. Frank's place is one of the bungalows opposite the fount in.'

'Cheers.'

The retirement community on the outskir s of Castlehead was comprised of several stree of purpose built bungalows. The leafy areas were well maintained. Andy could see there was a clubh use and bowling green. He knocked at the do of number 16.

The man who answered was tall and lear He wore a snazzy red shirt underneath a golfing jur per. 'Morning DS Calder, please come inside.'

Andy knew that Frank Maider was seventy ine years old, but judging by appearances he se ned younger. 'Thanks for seeing me at short notic Mr Maider.'

'Not at all, Detective Sergeant. I never stra far from my wee home these days.' Frank he ded straight for a small but functional kitchen. 'C p of tea?'

'Aye, please.'

'You're looking back into the Fau ner disappearance?' Frank glanced over his should r at his guest.

'That's right. We think the case may relate to a couple of murders we're investigating now.'

Frank gestured for Andy to take a seat in the lounge. 'I always thought that case would re its head again in the future.'

'Why is that, sir?'

'Because Joe Faulkner was a prominent me ber of the union back then, a real firebrand. His speeches were the cause of much of the industrial action and disturbance at Ferris Brewer during those years. My superior spat blood at the sound of his name.'

'So you thought there was more to his disappearance than a drunken encounter with some villains on the river bank?'

'Och, there was no evidence for it. Joe Faulkner just dropped off the radar after the 19th December '74. We'd no witness statements claiming to have set eyes on him from that date onwards. Not even his family. I assumed he was dead, especially with the number of enemies the man had. I just wished we could've found a body at least.'

'Enemies amongst the shipyard bosses, you mean?'

'Aye, and more besides. Joe was a drinker and a jack-the-lad.'

'Did you interview Joe's brother and sister-in-law in Portencross after the disappearance?'

'Aye, I spoke to them myself. A nice family. The other brother, Keith, he was a shifty type, but we couldn't ever pin anything on him. The folk at the farm were decent people. But none of them had seen the man for at least a month. There were dead ends everywhere you turned in that case.'

Andy sat back on the floral sofa and sipped his tea. 'You said Joe was a jack-the-lad. Any girlfriends on the scene?'

Frank glanced nervously about him, as if there may actually be someone else listening. 'There *was* a line of enquiry that I was pursuing at the time, but it was on the hush-hush. Based mostly on rumours I'd picked up.'

Andy clutched his mug tightly. 'Oh, aye?'

'We interviewed a few of Faulkner's workmates. They all kept talking about a young squeeze that Joe had back then. We're talking *very* young.'

Andy narrowed his eyes. '*Illegally* young?'

Frank whistled. 'Fifteen, maybe sixteen years old. I couldnae make a proper connection between this and his disappearance.' He put a veiny hand to his stomach. 'But I had a feeling this relationship was important. I just knew.'

'Surely a fifteen year old lassie couldn't have been responsible for the disappearance of a well-built thirty-five year old man?'

Frank shook his head. 'No, of course not. But it was who Joe's co-workers claimed the lassie *was* that sent little shivers down the back of my spine.'

'Who was she?'

'Only the daughter of one of the most powerful men in the shipworkers' union back then. He became the General Secretary, for Christ's sake. Joe must have met her through him, at a meeting in his house maybe. Whichever way it was, that relationship was a dangerous one for Faulkner to be pursuing. It was always my theory that the father found out and had him 'dealt with'. Of course I can never prove it. Then he was gunned down in the early eighties.' Frank lowered his voice to a whisper. 'It was only *Alec Duff's* daughter Joe was having it away with. That's why I expected this case to come around again one day. I can't recall the lassie's name, but I hear the Duffs had terrible problems with her after Joe was gone. Drugs and other stuff. Too much too young my Sheila always used to say.'

Andy was already on his feet. 'Nancy.'

'What was that?'

'Alec Duff's daughter is called Nancy.'

'Yes, that was it. Pretty name.'

'I'm sorry sir, but I'm going to have to get going.'

'No, that's fine. My visitors never tend to stay very long. I've got used to it.'

Chapter 45

Andy was jogging back to his car whilst talking to the boss on his mobile phone. They'd arranged to meet at Nancy McRae's house in Partick as soon as they could, with a squad car for back-up.

Dani was the first one to reach the property. She sat and waited for a couple of minutes, drumming her fingers on the steering wheel. 'Sod this,' she declared, climbing out and approaching the front door, knocking loudly when she reached it.

Nancy McRae opened up. 'Ah, visitors, visitors, please come in.'

Dani held up her warrant card. 'DCI Dani Bevan, Mrs McRae. I believe you've spoken with several members of my team.'

'Yes, that's right. Is DC Clifton not with you?' The woman peered over Dani's shoulder in mock expectation. 'That's who I'm usually fobbed off with.'

'It's just me today. Do you mind if I ask you a few questions?'

'Not at all.' Nancy led the way into a formal front sitting room. Dani sensed it wasn't used very often.

As the woman sat down and pulled up her sleeves, Dani noticed a series of faint needle scars spidering down Nancy's arms.

'It's a rather delicate matter, I'm afraid. Relating to something that happened in your past.'

Nancy's expression remained blank.

'Is it true that during the second half of 1974, when you were fifteen years old, you had a boyfriend called Joe Faulkner? He was considerably older than you.'

Nancy blinked several times. 'Well, I'm hardly likely to forget, am I? Joe was my first love – my only love if I'm being perfectly honest. Nobody ever compared to him afterwards.'

'How did you meet?'

'My father liked to have political meetings in our house. In the early days they involved dozens of sweaty, earnest young men squashed into our tiny front room. Joe was one of those men. I thought he was the most beautiful human being I'd ever set eyes on. It will be difficult to imagine now, but back then I was beautiful too. Although I was only fifteen, I had an intellect far beyond my years. Joe and I would debate issues for hours on end. He said I'd wind up being the Prime Minister.'

'Mr Duff didn't know about the relationship?'

'Not at first. But we intended to tell him, once I'd turned sixteen.' Nancy gave a hollow laugh. 'You may not believe it, but we planned to get married then.'

'This was before Joe went missing, in the December of that year?'

She nodded. 'The last time I ever saw him we made love in his flat. It was coming up to Christmas. Joe told me he was going to his brother's farm in Portencross to spend it with them. He said by the following year I'd be going there with him, as his wife.'

'What did you think had happened to him?'

'Well, I knew for certain that Joe wasn't killed on the night of the 19th.'

'How did you know?'

'Because I spoke to him after that date. He called me from a phonebox down the road from Crosbie Farm. That's how I know now they must have killed him. Because they always denied he'd ever been there that December.' She beat a fist against her chest. 'I know for definite he was.'

'Why didn't you tell the police this?'

Nancy smiled unpleasantly. 'I was fifteen years old. A schoolgirl. For starters, I knew they wouldn't take me seriously and if my parents found out I'd been sleeping with Joe then if he wasn't dead already Dad would have finished the job. But I still hoped he'd come back, you see? For those first few years I was longing for him to turn up on my doorstep. He could be unpredictable, have a roving eye. I thought he might be enjoying one last fling before settling down with me. If I admitted there'd been a sexual relationship between us, Joe would have gone straight to prison when he showed up.'

'But the months and years went past and he never did return.'

'No and I didn't handle it very well. I was a mess. I couldn't face school and played truant with some kids who got me into drugs. It helped me to deal with the pain. I actually don't think I could have got through those years without the heroin. But the stuff I had to do in order to get a fix I could've done without.'

'And Joe? Did you try to find him?'

Nancy cackled. 'The state I was in? But yes, in the early months I hung about at the Faulkners' place a lot. I knew Joe had been there and that they'd been lying about it. I kept banging on the door and shouting questions through the letterbox. Joe had told me he and his brother, Magnus, kept arguing. That Magnus wasn't prepared to help the strikers any more. It really hurt Joe. He felt like it was a betrayal. I started to suspect they'd done something to him. Then, one day in the height of summer, I got the bus out to the farm. I wasn't high or anything. I was quite clear-headed. The place was deserted. I asked in the village shop where they'd gone. The woman told me the family had emigrated.

Just like that. I knew then that they'd killed my Joe. Why else take off without telling anyone where hey were heading?'

'How long were you an addict, Nancy?'

'My dad finally got me into a rehabilitation u t in 1980. I was there just over a year. It saved my fe, I suppose.' Nancy raised her eyes from her lap. 'T at's how the American detective found me. Some ody showed him my records. He said my age fitte the person he was looking for.'

Dani had risen slowly to her feet. 'What d you mean?' Her heart was starting to pump hard.

'He got here about an hour before you di He was just making routine enquiries. The man dn't realise what he'd stumbled into.'

Dani made for the hallway, putting her hand out to touch the walls, navigating her way to the kit en, like a blind person in an unfamiliar place. ' am? Where are you, *Sam*?'

The silence was almost unbearable. Then she saw him on the floor by the back door. A p l of blood had seeped out onto the stone tiles fror his upper body.

Dani fell to her knees beside him. 'Oh, od. Please be alive. *Please*.' She put a hand to his eck, desperately seeking out a pulse.

There was a movement in the doorway b ind her. Dani turned, the tears staining her cheeks.

Nancy was standing absolutely still, holdi g a large knife in her hand. 'Don't worry, you'll so be joining him. I will make it quick, though. I prom e.'

Chapter 46

Before Nancy could take another step, Dani heard the noise of the flimsy front door being knocked off its hinges. The woman had time to turn briefly before the stream of heavy boots reached the kitchen and DC Calder flattened her to the ground, the knife she was holding falling with a clatter to one side of her prone form.

'Radio for an ambulance! Right Now!' Dani twisted back to Sam. She shuffled forward on her knees, feeling the cool blood seeping through her trousers.

Dani turned him over, trying to assess the extent of his injuries. She identified stab wounds across his chest, with some cuts having reached as high as his neck. She placed her hands over the areas where the bleeding seemed to be worse. 'Sam, can you hear me? The ambulance is coming. I'm here, my love, it's Dani. Please stay with me.'

Suddenly Andy was by her side. She watched him put his face up to the American's mouth and nose to listen for signs of breathing. Dani buried her head into Sam's chest whilst her friend and colleague performed some more basic medical checks, already knowing in her heart the stark words that were bound to follow.

'He's gone, Dani. I'm so sorry, but he's gone.'

*

DS Andy Calder's expression was a mask of concentration as he glared at a page which was densely packed with hand-written notes.

DS Alice Mann walked across the office floor to join him. 'Are you ready?'

'Aye, just give me a second. I want to make sure I'm thoroughly prepared.'

These were words she never thought she'd hear from Andy Calder. 'Come on, you've done enough. It's time.' He stood up squarely. 'You're probably right. Let's go.'

The pair didn't exchange a single word until they reached the interview room. Then Alice turned to her colleague and said, 'You take the lead. She's all yours.'

Nancy McRae was seated on the opposite side of the table with a female solicitor beside her and a half-drunk cup of tea resting in one hand.

'Good afternoon, Mrs McRae,' Andy began courteously. 'I hope you've been well taken care of by the duty staff?'

Nancy kept her eyes levelled at the blank wall behind her interrogators. 'Yes, well enough.'

'Good. Now, just a few wee questions to begin with.' He slid a pile of photographs towards his interviewee. 'Here's some shots of Sergeant Sam Sharpe of the Virginia Police Department, father of two, who'd given over thirty years of service to his country - after *you'd* had done with him.' Andy tapped the graphic images menacingly. 'Multiple stab wounds to the chest and stomach, defence wounds to both hands and arms. Our pathologist reckons you took him completely by surprise. He had no warning of the attack.'

Alice could tell that her colleague was finding it difficult to control his emotions. She didn't intervene. She'd take over if necessary, but not yet.

'Detective Sharpe bled to death on your grubby, cold kitchen floor, thousands of miles from home.

My only wish is that it was DCI Bevan's voice he heard in his ear before he slipped away and not *your* evil words.'

'Have you actually got a question, DS Calder?' The solicitor asked half-heartedly.

'We've got the knife that was used to butcher Detective Sharpe in our labs. Your fingerprints are all over it. Right now, my DCS is liaising with the Governor of Virginia. He's arranging for your extradition.'

Nancy slowly shifted her gaze. For the first time, her blank expression displayed a flicker of concern.

'Oh, had you not considered that possibility, Mrs McRae? Perhaps you also don't know that the State of Virginia has the death penalty for murder. And what they *really* don't like, over there in that beautiful part of the world, are people who carve up their law enforcement officers.'

'I'm still waiting for that question.' The solicitor folded her arms over her ample chest, looking as if she were going through the motions.

'Oh, it's coming, don't you worry. Now, I happen to know that you're responsible for the deaths of more people than just Detective Sharpe. So I'm going to make you an offer. Give me all the details of your other crimes and I might be able to organise for you to spend the rest of your miserable days rotting in a Scottish prison. Tell me nothing, and we'll let you taste justice American style. Did you know that in Virginia you can choose your own execution method? Lethal injection or the electric chair. Life's full of choices these days, isn't it?'

'I'll talk,' Nancy mumbled under her breath.

'Sorry, Mrs McRae, I didn't quite catch that?'

'I said, *I'll talk.*'

'Fair enough.' Andy turned to Alice. 'DS Mann, would you very kindly switch on the tape?'

Chapter 47

Professor Rhodri Morgan opened the front door of his second floor tenement flat. 'Good evening Detective, please come inside.'

'Is she okay to have visitors?' Andy stepped tentatively over the threshold. 'I can come back another time?'

'She's a little better. The doctor gave her a sedative but it's wearing off.'

Andy followed the professor into his grand sitting room, where the sun could be seen through the bay window, setting majestically over Kelvingrove Park. Dani was curled up in a blanket in one of the room's large armchairs, a mug of coffee cradled in her hands.

'Hi there,' Andy said softly, taking the chair opposite.

'Hi,' she replied, managing a glimmer of a smile.

'I can sling my hook if you want. Just say the word.'

'No, I want you to be here.'

Rhodri entered with a mug of coffee for Andy. He placed it on a side table and slipped out again.

'We've been interviewing solidly for the last two days.'

'Did she talk?'

Andy nodded solemnly. 'Yes, she talked.'

'I want to know everything.'

'Are you sure? This can wait until you're feeling better, more recovered.'

Dani shook her head vigorously. 'No, it can't. I *need* to know.'

Andy took a deep breath and picked up his mug.

'When she got out of rehab, Nancy tried to rebuild her life. Her father got her an admin job at the union offices and things seemed back on track for a while. Then the Ferris Brewer workers went out on strike in '82. Alec Duff visited the front line to offer his support.'

'And one of his own union members shot him in the head.'

'Yeah, I reckon that was when Nancy really lost the plot. She married Tony McRae a few years later and the two of them bought their place in Partick. The pair lived a normal existence on the surface. But Nancy was obsessed with finding out what happened to Joe Faulkner. Her father was dead and buried, but there was still a faint hope that she could be reunited with Joe once more.

She knew the family had moved abroad. Nancy isn't stupid, she assumed wherever it was must be English-speaking. She figured the US or Australia. That was her only starting point. Like the inhabitants of Portencross, Nancy had no idea that Vicki had stayed behind in Scotland. The woman didn't have access to any police reports or travel records, so she'd not a great deal to go on.'

'It was an impossible task, surely?'

'For a good number of years it really was. Then the internet came along and Nancy's job got a little bit easier.'

Dani shuffled up with interest.

'She figured that at some point, one of the Faulkners, or their descendants, would need to have some kind of contact with Portencross again, whether it was to go to a funeral, or simply satisfy their curiosity. Nancy judged that after a certain number of years had passed, one of them might slip up and try to come back.'

'It was a smart theory.'

'So Nancy joined a series of online communities that were related to Portencross and the surrounding area - these included book clubs, travel blogs and genealogy sites. That's how she came across the McNeils. John was constantly posting stuff about his research into the McNeil of Portencross. Then, about two years ago, John shared his excitement at discovering there was another prominent Scottish family, interconnected to his own and with members living right there in his home own of Richmond, Virginia.'

'The Faulkners.'

'As soon as Nancy saw the name, she knew she'd found them. She immediately got in contact with McNeil through the discussion forum and claimed she was one of the McNeil clan, keen to hear further updates. Of course, John had absolutely no idea that these requests were bogus, why should he? You can pretend to be anyone you want on these sites. Nobody checks.'

'Bloody internet.'

'Nancy got hold of the McNeils' address in Richmond from these conversations. But most crucially, John McNeil told her about Detective Dale Faulkner and how they all might be able to play happy families in the future.'

'So when Dale killed the McNeils, thinking that was the end of anyone rooting around into his past in Scotland, Nancy had already found out his whereabouts.'

'Yep. But Nancy had a problem. Back in 2014, she was diagnosed with cancer. The recovery process was invasive and tough. Tony insisted she have every treatment available. She was out of action for the best part of eighteen months. When she finally able to get back on her computer and find out what was going on with the McNeils, she encountered radio silence. The guy hadn't posted a thing for the whole time she'd been ill.'

'That's because he was dead.'

'Aye, but Nancy didn't know that. When she felt recovered enough, Mrs McRae took a trip. She told Tony she needed to recuperate in the sun for a few weeks. By this point she was tutoring freelance from home, having given up her lecturing job for her treatment. There was nothing to stop her finally completing her mission. She had the McNeils' address and knew that Dale was a cop, but that was it.'

'She travelled to Richmond.'

'Nancy went straight to the McNeils' house. She found the place boarded up and abandoned but easy enough to get inside. This was when she started to get suspicious about what might have happened to the pair. Nancy found the chained up freezer in the basement and got a bad feeling. The woman already believed the Faulkners were murderers, so it wasn't any great leap to assume that Dale had got rid of the old couple.'

'Is that when she contacted Dale?'

Andy nodded. 'She sent him a few anonymous letters, just to rattle him up. They suggested he may have left a couple of corpses on ice.'

'Dale must have panicked. That was when he shifted the bodies and buried them?'

'But Nancy wanted to find out what had become of Joe, she wasn't interested in bringing Dale to justice for the murders of John and Rita. She also wanted to get this information without ending up in a Virginian prison cell.'

'So she came up with the idea of the 911 call from the McNeils' place?'

'Nancy's father had some old contacts in Pittsburgh, going back decades. One of these contacts was a businessman of the shadier variety. He got hold of a gun for her. All Nancy wanted at this stage was to make Dale talk. She needed a weapon to threaten him with. The intention was to have a discussion. She'd even set out some candles in bottles, to make the scene more conducive. But when she'd lured Dale to that house, set eyes on him for the first time in all those years, Nancy was overcome with rage. She forced Dale to sit at the table and asked him repeatedly where his uncle was, what had happened to him. Dale wouldn't tell her and the clock was ticking, so she shot him.'

'That was her first kill. It must have felt good. Justice for Joe after all those years.'

'Yes, but she still didn't know the truth. Nancy wanted more. Before she fled from the house and dumped the gun in the James River, Nancy went through Dale's wallet. Inside, she found a folded up flyer for a classical music concert in New York City from the previous year. It was showcasing a solo performance by the famous Scottish pianist, Vicki Kendrick. She'd never made the connection before. Now the pieces had slotted into place.'

'Nancy had found Dale's sister. So it wasn't Sam who led her to Vicki. That's some comfort at least.'

'It was time for Nancy to come home.'

Dani screwed up her face. 'It mustn't have been long after his wife got back from the US that Tony McRae had his accident. That can't be a coincidence?'

'Oh, it isn't. Nancy returned a few days before she was expected. Tony was in their bed with one of the secretaries from the shipyard. He'd been shagging her since Nancy had been diagnosed with cancer. She'd always known he was a useless piece of crap, but Nancy decided he might finally be able to serve a purpose. That Thursday evening, when he'd gone into work late, to check his team's handiwork on the order that was approaching its deadline, Nancy followed him.'

'And shoved her husband off the platform onto the ship's steel hull, 120 feet below. I suppose now she'd already killed a man, it was becoming easy.'

'Nancy used her husband's death to launch a campaign against Hemingway Shipyard for negligence.'

'So what about Vicki?'

'Nancy said that befriending Vicki was fairly straightforward. She hung about the bars around St Mungo's college and struck up a conversation with her. Vicki was lonely and possessed a pathological fear of being left on her own in the dark. Nancy went to Vicki's place quite often and they drank together, sometimes they made love. Vicki thought that was the price she had to pay for the company. She believed that was why Nancy had picked her up in the first place. Vicki didn't want the neighbours to know she had a female lover, so Nancy came in through the back.'

'What happened on the afternoon Vicki was killed?'

'Nancy was due to come over for a drink before Vicki's performance. She said it was easy. Vicki was as light as a feather. Nancy let her drink the best part of a bottle of wine before she strung her up to the light fitting in the sitting room, inviting the woman to tell her exactly what they'd done with Joseph Faulkner. Every time she refused to do so, Nancy stabbed her with a kitchen knife.'

'And did Vicki confess?'

'Partially. She admitted he was dead and that they'd buried his body somewhere on the farm. But the woman bled out before Nancy could get the whole story. She'd nicked the carotid artery by mistake. After that, Vicki was a goner.'

Dani sighed deeply. 'Five people dead, all to keep that family's secret.' The tears started to leak out again onto her pale cheeks.

Andy put his cup down and knelt in front of his boss, taking her hands. 'I could call James. Get him to come back right now. I know he would. He loves you.'

'I can't let him see me like this, it wouldn't be fair. It would break his heart. I just need some more time, that's all.'

'Okay, but promise me you won't push him away. You haven't lost everything, please remember that.'

'Then why does it feel as if I have?' Dani crumpled into sobs.

Andy leant forward and took her in his arms. 'You've got to be strong, Ma'am. In time, it will get better.'

Chapter 48

If they weren't standing in the centre of the valley watching several enormous diggers demolishing a set of perfectly good new-builds, it would have been quite a pleasant view.

DCS Douglas pulled up in a shiny new BMW and climbed out. He gazed about him with a grim expression. 'You certainly know how to piss off people in high places, DCI Bevan. The DCC had just put a deposit down on one of these houses for his daughter.'

Calder burst out laughing, he couldn't help himself.

To his great surprise, Ronnie Douglas smiled too. 'But then again, fuck him.'

Dani chuckled, pulling her jacket more tightly around her thinner frame. She'd lost a bit of weight in the previous couple of months and it was beginning to show.

'How many of these houses will they have to pull down, do you think?'

'We'll keep going until the specialist team from forensic anthropology discover the remains, sir.'

'Do you *really* think we'll find his body?'

Dani looked about her at the otherwise peaceful landscape, imaging what it would have been like when the Crosbie Farm had still stood in that spot. 'Yes, I do. It's only been forty years, his bones won't have disappeared. We'll find Joseph Faulkner and give him a proper burial.'

'Have we got any real idea how he died?'

'Hopefully the anthropologists can tell us more

when they've got the remains to work on. My theory is that Joe and Magnus argued. Farms are full of potential weapons. It could have been a spade or even a shotgun. Magnus took action to defend himself and his brother wound up dead. The family were there at the farmhouse for Christmas and they helped to get rid of the evidence. It's lonely up here and remote. I expect they didn't think anyone would discover what they'd done.'

'But they didn't count on Nancy Duff hounding them with questions about her missing lover. She knew something had happened at the farm that Christmas. It was her persistence that drove the Faulkners out of Portencross,' Andy explained. 'I reckon they borrowed money from Mac, the guy who owned the garage, so that they could pay for their flights and visas to get into the US. They weren't fleeing because they owed him money; they used Mac's money in order to get away. Duff wouldn't have stopped until she'd brought the polis to their door.'

'She still found them in the end.' Dani stared off into the distance.

'How is the prosecution proceeding?' Andy turned to address his superior officer.

'We're still in negotiations with the US government. They want Nancy Duff tried over there for Sergeant Sharpe's murder. I think that eventually they'll get their way.'

Dani flicked her head back round. 'What about the deal Calder and Mann made with Duff?'

Andy shrugged his shoulders. 'It wasn't recorded on the tape. I spoke with the duty solicitor who was there with us. Her son's on the police training programme. She's not going to kick up a stink.'

Dani walked away from her colleagues, she didn't have the strength to argue the point with them. As she moved further from the noise of the diggers, Dani heard a car engine approach. It was James in his sporty hatchback. He pulled up at the kerb and got out. Dani smiled at him.

'Hey gorgeous, how is the wanton destruction of perfectly good housing stock coming along?'

'Very well, actually. We should have set the country's economy back by at least a couple of points by the end of the day.'

James wrapped her up in his arms. 'Good work, detective. Another productive day at the office.'

Dani couldn't help but chuckle.

'Now, a little bird told me that you wouldn't be needed for a few hours and I could whisk you away for a gourmet lunch.'

'Ah, I see. That little bird doesn't happen to weigh around thirteen stone and answer to the name of Andy Calder by any chance?'

James made a poker face. 'Might do.'

Dani slipped her arm around his back and proceeded to guide him towards the car. 'Come on then, show me the bright lights of West Kilbride.'

'Actually, I was thinking we could maybe go into the city. You know these provincial places aren't entirely my scene.'

'I can't be late back. The team might find something while I'm gone.'

'If they do, I'm sure they'll be in touch. In the meantime, let's just concentrate on stuffing our faces, okay?'

'Sure.' Dani nodded, swallowing down the tiny lump threatening to expand in her throat and keeping it at bay with a wide grin. 'Let's do that, partner.'

Chapter 49
Crosbie Farm, West Kilbride,
Christmas 1974

Magnus Faulkner was shovelling manure in one of the larger of his animal sheds. The forecast that weekend was for snow. He wanted to bring his cattle inside before the weather turned.

The stark strip lighting which ran along the roof of the shed was making his eyes ache. Magnus had been working since five that morning. He was exhausted. But at least he'd managed to get a tree down from the forest for the weans to decorate.

Magnus heard the sound of a car engine outside on the track that led to the main road into Portencross. He knew it would be his brothers, Keith and Joe. His heart sank. They'd been out shopping in West Kilbride. He wasn't much looking forward to seeing either of them. Let alone having them at the farm during the entire holidays.

The corrugated iron door creaked open. A tall, dark-haired man entered; his presence powerful and commanding, especially compared to his worn down older brother, stooped awkwardly over his shovel.

'Evening, Magnus.' Joe Faulkner had a broad smile on his handsome face.

The farmer peered over the shoulder of his youngest sibling. 'Where's Keith?'

'I dropped him off at a bar in Seamill. He's planning to get a cab back here later on.'

Magnus tutted. It was bloody typical. Keith would be absolutely plastered by then and might very well wake Sue and the kids as he blundered in. Not to mention the fact he'd been trying to avoid being alone with Joe since they'd both arrived. '*Great.*'

'Och, it's the festive season, Magnus. You've got to allow folk to enjoy themselves.'

'All Keith ever does is *enjoy himself.* Now, pick up one of those shovels and help me shift this cow shit.'

Reluctantly, Joe did as he was told. The two men worked in silence for a while. Then Joe straightened up. 'Have you managed to get those Christmas relief boxes prepared for me yet?'

Magnus sighed, knowing this was coming, sooner or later. 'I've barely enough to feed my own family, Joe. It's a bad time of the year. We've just bought the presents for Dale and Vic. It was bloody expensive.'

'But you're talking about *extras* there, Magnus. Those men up at the shipyards are struggling even to put food on the table for their weans.'

'If you had your own children, you'd know that providing them with Christmas presents isn't a sodding *extra.*'

Joe took a deep breath. 'There are bigger issues at stake here than whether Vicki gets a new Barbie doll. We've asked those boys to go out on strike because it's to protect the industry for future generations. The least I can do in return is give them a helping hand to feed their families.'

Magnus took a step closer, feeling the anger rising in his chest. 'But it's not you who's doing that, it's *me.* Why do all your great causes involve other people having to make sacrifices, it's never *you,* though is it?'

'That's not true. I'm a worker, just like all the men I represent.' Joe puffed himself up with pride.

'But that's not strictly accurate, is it brother? The union gives you extra for being their man on the shopfloor. I happen to know for certain that Alec Duff makes sure you're not out of pocket.'

Joe narrowed his eyes. 'It's complicated, Magnus. You don't understand how the system works.'

'And all you can do in return is to shag the man's fifteen year old daughter – just a wean herself!' Magnus was practically shouting now, the sweat running off his brow despite the bitter chill.

'Who told you that?' Joe's tone was level and steely.

'Keith. He came to pick you up from your flat once and saw the girl leaving. He recognised her. We all know Duff's family. There's only one reason a young lassie goes to a man's flat on her own - especially if *you're* the man. What would our Ma have said about that? It would've killed her.'

Joe had started sweating too. 'It's not like that. I love Nancy. When she turns sixteen we're going to get married. We just need to make sure her Da doesn't find out first.'

'Do you really think the lassie turning sixteen will make any difference? Alec Duff will know straight off that you've been knobbing his daughter since she was still in gym slips. He's hardly going to let you get away with that.' Magnus almost laughed.

'Alec is fond of me. He says I'm like a son to him!'

'Then it's bloody incest, too!' Magnus threw his shovel to the concrete floor with a clatter. 'You people are so full of shit. You come here all high and mighty about the principles of the strike when you've got no feckin' principles of your own. Forget it. You'll get no more food parcels from me – I'm looking after my own kin from now on. You're no longer a part of it.' He turned to walk back towards the house.

Joe charged forward and gave his brother a shove from behind. 'You can't do that! I've promised them!'

Magnus lost his footing and fell to his knees on the concrete, putting his hands straight into a pile of straw and cow shit. 'It wasn't your promise to make. Don't you understand that?'

Joe stood stock still over his brother's crouched

form. 'I know people, Magnus. Alec Duff knows people. If you back out now, I won't be able to protect you, or Sue and the kids.'

Magnus couldn't believe what he was hearing. Still on his hands and knees he tried to absorb Joe's chilling words. The farmer's head rose up. Directly in front of him, leaning against the far wall of the shed was his shotgun.

The image of that gun was still imprinted on the retina of his eyes when the entire building was plunged into darkness.

'What the fuck?' Joe Faulkner blustered, perhaps unused to the sudden power cuts that the more remote areas of Scotland suffered on a pretty much daily basis.

Magnus's actions were not driven by any conscious thought process but by a strong, almost animalistic instinct. He remained on all fours and crawled forward in the darkness until he knew he'd got as far as the wall. He reached out with his filthy hands until they were gripping the barrel firmly.

The farmer clambered to his feet and turned. His eyes were slowly adjusting to the gloom but he still couldn't make out anything distinct.

'Magnus, where are you?' The words were shrill and panicky.

He directed the gun towards the sound of Joe's voice. Somehow, not being able to see his victim properly helped Magnus to do the job. If he'd been able to look into his brother's eyes, he may not have possessed the balls to do it.

Magnus pulled the trigger. The noise was ten times louder than he was expecting, although he'd set off shots dozens of times before. It was something about the darkness, which seemed to amplify all of his senses.

He heard Joe's body fall to the ground. Pieces of

his brain and flesh had sprayed onto Magnus, reaching him even from where he was standing, at the other side of the shed.

He knew his brother was dead.

The only question now was what they would need to do next.

If you enjoyed this novel, please take a few moments to write a brief review. Reviews really help to introduce new readers to my books and this allows me to keep on writing.
Many thanks,

Katherine.

If you would like to find out more about my books and read my reviews and articles then please visit my blog, TheRetroReview at:

www.KatherinePathak.wordpress.com

To find out about new releases and special offers follow me on Twitter:

@KatherinePathak

Most of all, thanks for reading!

Made in the US,
San Bernardino, (
11 October 201(